"Ragnar Jónasson's *Snowblind* is as dazzling a novel as its title implies and the wonderful Ari Thór is a welcome addition to the pantheon of Scandinavian detectives. I can't wait until the sequel!"
—William Ryan, author of the Captain Alexei Korolev series

"A truly chilling debut, perfect for fans of Karin Fossum and Henning Mankell."
—Eva Dolan, author of *Long Way Home*

"An isolated community, subtle clueing, clever misdirection, and more than a few surprises combine to give a modern-day Golden Age whodunit. Well done! I look forward to the next in the series."
—Dr. John Curran, author of *The Mass*

"*Snowblind* brings you the chill of a snowbound Icelandic fishing village cut off from the outside world, and the warmth of a really well-crafted and -translated murder mystery."
—Michael Ridpath, author of the Power and Money thrillers

"The complex characters and absorbing plot make *Snowblind* memorable. Its setting—Siglufjördur, a small fishing village isolated in the depths of an Icelandic winter—makes it unforgettable. Let's hope that more of this Icelandic author's work will be translated."
—Sandra Balzo, author of the Maggy Thorsen mysteries

"In Ari Thór Arason, Nordic noir has a new hero as compelling and interesting as the northern Icelandic setting."   —Nick Quantrill, author of the Joe Geraghty series

"If a Golden Age crime novel were to emerge from a literary deep freeze, then you'd hope it would read like this. Jónasson cleverly squeezes this small, isolated town in northern Iceland until it is hard to breathe, ensuring the setting is as claustrophobic as any locked

room. If you call your book *Snowblind,* then you better make sure it's chilling. He does."
—Craig Robertson, author
of the Forever series

"If Arnaldur is the King and Yrsa the Queen of Icelandic crime fiction, then Ragnar is surely the Crown Prince . . . more, please!"
—Karen Meek, *Euro Crime*

"Ragnar Jónasson brilliantly evokes the claustrophobia of small-town Iceland in this intriguing murder mystery. Let's hope this is the first of many translations by Quentin Bates."   —Zoë Sharp, author of the Charlie Fox thrillers

"Ragnar Jónasson is simply brilliant at planting a hook and using the magic of a dark Icelandic winter to reel in the story. *Snowblind* screams isolation and darkness in an exploration of the basic Icelandic nature with all its attendant contrasts and extremes, amid a plot filled with twists, turns, and one surprise after another."
—Jeffrey Siger, author of the
Chief Inspector Andreas Kaldis mysteries

"A chilling, thrilling slice of Icelandic noir."   —Thomas Enger, author of the Henning Juul series

"A stunning murder mystery set in the northernmost town in Iceland, written by one of the country's finest crime writers. Ragnar has Nordic noir down pat—a remote small-town mystery that is sure to please crime fiction aficionados."   —Yrsa Sigurdardóttir, author of the Thora Gudmundsdóttir series

"*Snowblind* is a brilliantly crafted crime story that gradually unravels old secrets in a small Icelandic town . . . an excellent debut from a talented Icelandic author. I can't wait to read more."
—Sarah Ward, author of the Inspector Francis Sadler series

"Is King Arnaldur Indridason looking to his laurels? There is a young pretender beavering away, his eye on the crown: Ragnar Jónasson."
—Barry Forshaw, author of *Nordic Noir: The Pocket Essential Guide to Scandinavian Crime Fiction, Film, and TV*

"An intricately plotted crime novel, *Snowblind* is a remarkable debut. Ragnar Jónasson has delivered an intelligent whodunit that updates, stretches, and redefines the locked-room mystery format. The author's cool, clean prose constructs atmospheric word pictures that re-create the harshness of an Icelandic winter in the reader's mind. Destined to be an instant classic."
—*EuroDrama*

"*Snowblind* is a beautifully written thriller, as tense as it is terrifying—Jónasson is a writer with a big future."
—Luca Veste, author of *The Dying Place*

"It sometimes feels as if everyone in Iceland is writing crime novels, but the first appearance of Ragnar Jónasson in English translation (itself a fluid adaptation by British mystery writer Quentin Bates) is cause for celebration."
—Maxim Jakubowski, *Love Reading*

"*Snowblind* has given rise to one of the biggest buzzes in the crime fiction world, and refreshingly usurps the cast-iron grip of the present obsession with domestic noir . . . a complex and perplexing case, in a claustrophobic and chilling setting."
—*Raven Crime Reads*

"The intricate plotting is reminiscent of the great Christie, though the setting is very much more modern and darker. There is an increasing tension and threat that mirrors the developing snowstorm and creates a sense of isolation and confinement, ensuring that the story develops strongly once the characters and scene are laid out."
—*Live Many Lives*

"A brooding, atmospheric book; with the darkness and constant snow, there is a claustrophobic feel to everything, which is heightened to the nth degree when there is an avalanche and the one road in and out of the village is blocked." —*Reading Writes* and *For Reading Addicts*

"It is surely only a matter of time before *Snowblind* and the rest of Ragnar's Dark Iceland series go on to take the Nordic noir genre by storm. The rest of the world has been patiently waiting for a new author to emerge from Iceland and join the ranks of Indridason and Sigurdardóttir and it appears that he is now here."
—Grant Nichol, *Volcanic Lilypad*

"Jónasson's prose throughout this entire novel is captivating, and frequently borders on the poetic, constructing something that is both beautiful and uncomfortable for the reader . . . a simply stunning piece of prose that will certainly put him in the thick of the crime genre in the United Kingdom." —*Mad Hatter Reviews*

"*Snowblind* uses its stunningly beautiful yet brutally remote setting to create a chilling, atmospheric locked-room mystery. Ragnar Jónasson is an outstanding new voice in Nordic noir."
—*Crime Thriller Girl*

"Dark Iceland? This man not only invented it, he rules it. From the opening page, the tension and chilling horror is there. The idyllic snow angel image is no longer full of childhood innocence and the snowblind of the title covers your eyes with white flurries and clouds of mist that shroud the mystery and intrigue." —*The Booktrail*

"*Snowblind* is a subtle, quiet mystery set in the most exquisite landscape—a slow burner that will suck you in and not let you go until you finish the final page." —*Reading Room with a View*

"A damn good thriller." —*OMG That Book*

"The plot twists and turns as the investigation uncovers a plethora of old deceits and current intrigues. Festering wounds are opened spilling secrets as dark as the days, as shocking as the blood on the suffocating snow." —*Never Imitate*

"There is something almost hauntingly melancholic about this story. The claustrophobia felt by Ari Thór is palpable. You can almost feel the walls of snow caging you in and the sense of perpetual winter darkness makes you reach for the light switch." —*From First Page to Last*

"Jónasson has bestowed his characters with unique, more importantly believable, personalities, and has made sure that their interactions throughout serve mainly to play on the reader's mind and psychology." —*Book Fabulous*

"Ragnar Jónasson's debut *Snowblind* is a brilliant new thriller with storytelling that is clear and crisp. . . . The plot twists and turns as the tension and intensity builds and we are treated to an excellent ending." —*Liz Loves Books*

"The small-town mentality juxtaposes with the vastness of the landscape and lends an eeriness to the overall narrative. The prose is delightful with moments of exceptional clarity." —*Bleach House Library*

"If you like cold and claustrophobic settings as I do, then this might just be the book for you. Jónasson does a wonderful job placing you right there in the small snowed-in town." —Rebecca Bradley, author of the Detective Inspector Hannah Robbins series

"A tiny, segregated town is a superb setting for a crime novel, and Jónasson exploits it well. He builds a layered mystery featuring a series of unhealthy secrets, and past crimes buried deep in the sheltered, almost claustrophobic recesses of family life, which Ari Thór will pay a high price for unravelling."   —*Thriller Books Journal*

"If the rest of the Dark Iceland series is as accomplished as *Snowblind*, Ragnar Jónasson's name is poised to become as common place as that of Stieg Larsson's. Don't be fooled into thinking Jónasson is a mere imitation. By deconstructing the Golden Age traditional mystery within a foreign setting, Ragnar Jónasson has practically created his own genre. For lack of a better term, let's call this cozy noir."
          —*BOLO Books*

"Siglufjördur is a thriller writer's dream location—a tight-knit community, encircled by mountains, almost round-the-clock darkness in midwinter, cut off from the rest of the country by the harsh weather; it all adds to the brooding menace of having a killer at large!"   —*Our Reviews Blogspot*

"*Snowblind*—a master class in scene setting and subtle tension building . . . Where Agatha Christie created a murder mystery with a small suspect pool on a fast moving train or within a large country house, Ragnar Jónasson creates the same feel in a whole town."
          —*Grab This Book*

"Siglufjördur is a wonderfully evocative setting; encircled by mountains and cut off in the winter when the roads are impassable, as the complex web of secrets becomes ever more enmeshed, its small-town, suffocating darkness heightens Ari Thór's increasing paranoia at being an outsider in his own land."   —*Claire Thinking*

"This is a first outing in English for Ari Thór, bolstered by a pin-sharp translation by Quentin Bates. Jónasson evokes an almost timeless feel to his narrative, with only mobile phones and computers reminding us that this is the twenty-first century. It's no surprise, either, to discover that Jónasson has translated fourteen Agatha Christie novels into Icelandic, as *Snowblind* has echoes of Golden Age stories. Siglufjördur may be light-years away from St. Mary Mead, but villagers here have secrets to hide."

—Sharon Wheeler, *The Times* (London)

"*Snowblind* is as atmospheric a murder mystery as you could find."

—*For Winter Nights*

"An entertaining—and curiously thought-provoking—addition to Icelandic noir. The writer manages the feat of keeping the prose quite pacey while getting across the ennui of the town's bleak existence during the harsh winter."

—*Café Thinking*

"Beautifully written . . . plenty of twists and turns."

—*Bibliophile Book Club*

"Ragnar Jónasson is a new name in the crime-writing genre and I urge anyone who is a fan of Nordic crime noir to rush out and get a copy of *Snowblind*. This you will want to add to your collection. It is really that good . . . a tense, gripping novel."

—*The Last Word*

NIGHTBLIND

Also by Ragnar Jónasson

Snowblind

Nightblind

RAGNAR JÓNASSON

translated by Quentin Bates

Minotaur Books

A Thomas Dunne Book
New York

A THOMAS DUNNE BOOK FOR MINOTAUR BOOKS.
An imprint of St. Martin's Press.

NIGHTBLIND. Copyright © 2015 by Ragnar Jónasson. Translation copyright © 2016 by Quentin Bates. All rights reserved. Printed in the United States of America. For information, address St. Martin's Press, 175 Fifth Avenue, New York, N.Y. 10010.

www.thomasdunnebooks.com
www.minotaurbooks.com

Maps copyright © 2015 by Ólafur Valsson

Library of Congress Cataloging-in-Publication Data

Names: Ragnar Jónasson, 1976– author. | Bates, Quentin, translator.
Title: Nightblind : a thriller / Ragnar Jónasson ; translated by Quentin Bates.
Other titles: Nattblinda. English
Description: First U.S. edition. | New York : Minotaur Books, 2017. | "A Thomas Dunne Book."
Identifiers: LCCN 2017025691 | ISBN 9781250096098 (hardcover) | ISBN 9781250096104 (ebook)
Subjects: LCSH: Murder—Investigation—Iceland—Fiction. | Police—Iceland—Fiction. | GSAFD: Psychological fiction. | Suspense fiction.
Classification: LCC PT7511.R285 N3813 2017 | DDC 839/.6934—dc23
LC record available at https://lccn.loc.gov/2017025691

Our books may be purchased in bulk for promotional, educational, or business use. Please contact your local bookseller or the Macmillan Corporate and Premium Sales Department at 1-800-221-7945, extension 5442, or by email at MacmillanSpecialMarkets@macmillan.com.

First published in Iceland under the title Náttblinda by Veröld

Previously published in Great Britain by Orenda Books

First U.S. Edition: December 2017

10 9 8 7 6 5 4 3 2 1

To Natalía, from Dad

Acknowledgments

The author would like to thank the people of Siglufjördur for their wonderful setting, and would like to point out that the characters and the story are entirely fictional. Grateful thanks are due to prosecutor Hulda María Stefánsdóttir for her invaluable insight into police work. I would also like to thank the city of Stockholm's cultural programme for the use of a guest apartment at Villa Bergshyddan, where *Nightblind* was partly written.

The events of *Nightblind* take place approximately five years after *Snowblind*. Ari Thór Arason is still working as a police officer in the small town of Siglufjördur. Tómas, his boss, has moved down south, to the capital city of Reykjavík. The new inspector is a man called Herjólfur. Ari Thór has been reunited with his girlfriend Kristín, and they now have a ten-month-old son.

The next book in the series, *Blackout*, picks up the story again directly after the events of *Snowblind*, with the following two books set to complete the series of events linking *Snowblind* and *Nightblind*.

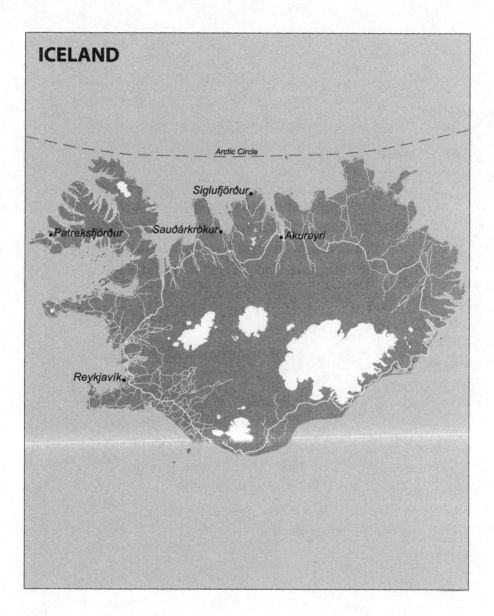

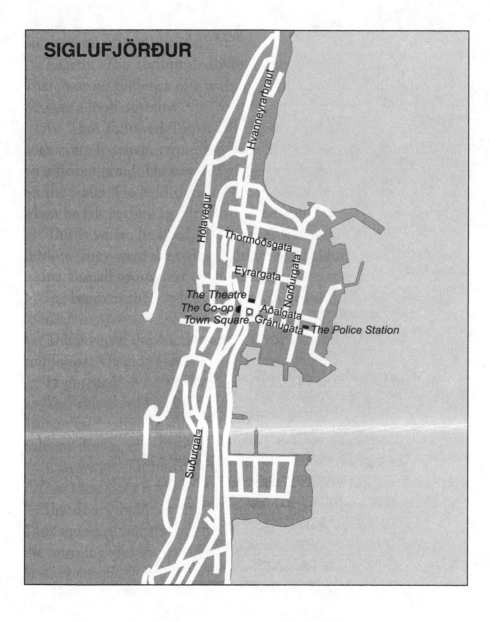

Something goes astray
In men and weather,
Men and words…

From the poem 'Broken', by Þorsteinn frá Hamri
(Skessukatlar, 2013)

Unsettling.

Yes, that's the word. There was something unsettling about that ancient, broken-down house. The walls were leaden and forbidding, especially in this blinding rain. Autumn felt more like a state of mind than a real season here. Winter had swiftly followed on the heels of summer in late September or early October, and it was as if autumn had been lost somewhere on the road north. Herjólfur, Siglufjördur's police inspector, didn't particularly miss it, at least not the autumn he knew from Reykjavík, where he had been brought up. He had come to appreciate the summer in Siglufjördur, with its dazzlingly bright days. He enjoyed the winter as well, with its all-enveloping darkness that curled itself around you like a giant cat.

The house stood a little way from the entrance to the Strákar tunnel and as far as Herjólfur had been able to work out, it was years since anyone had lived in the place, located some distance from where the town proper hugged the shoreline. It looked as if it had simply been left there for nature's heavy hands to do as she wished with the place, and her handiwork had been brutal.

Herjólfur had a special interest in this abandoned building and it was something that worried him. He was rarely fearful, having trained himself to push uncomfortable feelings to one side, but this time he'd been unsuccessful, and he was far from happy. The patrol car was now parked by the side of the road, and Herjólfur was hesitant to leave it. He shouldn't even have been on duty, but Ari Thór, the town's other police officer, was down with flu.

Herjólfur sat still for a moment, the patrol car lashed by the bitter chill of the rain. His thoughts travelled to the warm living room at home. Moving up here had been something of a culture shock, but he and his wife had managed to make themselves comfortable, and their simple house had been gradually transformed into a home. Their daughter was at university in Reykjavík; their son had remained with his parents, living in the basement and attending a local college.

Herjólfur had a few days' holiday coming up, assuming Ari Thór was fit to return to work. He had been planning to surprise his wife with a break in Reykjavík. He had booked flights from Akureyri and secured a couple of theatre tickets. This was the type of thing he tried to make a habit, to take a rest from the day-to-day routine whenever the opportunity presented itself. Now, in the middle of the night, and while he was still on duty, he fixed his mind on the upcoming trip, as if using it as a lifeline to convince himself that everything would be fine when he entered the house.

His mind wandered back to his wife. They had been married for twenty-two years. She had become pregnant early in the relationship, and so they were married soon after. There hadn't been any hesitation or, indeed, choice. The decision wasn't anything to do with faith, but more with the traditions of decency to which he clung. He had been properly brought up – a stern believer in the importance of setting a good example. And they were in love, of course. He'd never have married a woman he didn't love. Then their daughter was born and she became the apple of his eye. She was in her twenties now, studying psychology, even though he had tried to convince her to go in for law. That was a path that could have brought her to work with the police, connected in some way to the world of law and order; his world.

The boy had come along three years later. Now he was nineteen, a stolid and hard-working lad in his final year at college. Maybe he'd be the one to go in for law, or just apply straight to the police college.

Herjólfur had done his best to make things easier for them. He had plenty of influence in the force and he'd happily pull strings on their behalf if they decided to choose that kind of future; he was also guiltily aware that he was often inclined to push a little too hard. But he was proud of his children and it was his dearest hope that they would feel the same about him. He knew that he had worked hard, had pulled himself and his family up to a comfortable position in a tough environment. There was no forgetting that the job came with its own set of pressures.

The family had emerged from the financial crash in a bad way, with practically every penny of their savings having gone up in smoke overnight. Those were tough days, with sleepless nights, his nerves on edge and an unremitting fear that cast a shadow over everything. Now, at long last, things seemed to have started to stabilise again; he had what appeared to be a decent position in this new place, and they were comfortable, even secure. Although neither of them had mentioned it, he knew that Ari Thór had applied for the inspector's post as well. Ari Thór had a close ally in Tómas, the former inspector at the Siglufjördur station, who had since moved to a new job in Reykjavík. Herjólfur wasn't without connections of his own, but Tómas's heartfelt praise of and support for Ari Thór hadn't boded well. And yet, the post had gone to him and not to Ari Thór – a young man of whom Herjólfur still hadn't quite got the measure. Ari Thór had not proved to be particularly talkative and it wasn't easy to work out what he was thinking. Herjólfur wasn't sure if there was a grudge there over the way things had turned out. They hadn't been working together for long. Ari Thór's son had been born at the end of the previous year, on Christmas Eve, and he had gone on to take four months' paternity leave plus a month's holiday. They weren't friends or even that friendly, but it was still early days.

Herjólfur's senses sharpened, and all thoughts of his colleague were pushed from his mind as he stepped out of the car, and gradually approached the house. He had that feeling again. *The feeling that something was very wrong.*

If it came to it, he reckoned he could easily hold his own with one man; two would be too much for him now that age had put paid to the fitness of his earlier years. He shook his head, as if to clear away ungrounded suspicions. There was every chance the old place would be empty. He was surprised at his discomfort.

There was no traffic. Few people found reason to travel to Siglufjördur at this time of year, least of all in the middle of the night and in such foul weather. The official first day of winter, according to the old Icelandic calendar, was next weekend, but that would only confirm what everyone already knew up here in the north – winter had arrived.

Herjólfur stopped in his tracks, suddenly aware of a beam of light – torchlight? – inside the old building. So there *was* someone there in the shadows, maybe more than one. Herjólfur was becoming increasingly dubious about this call-out and his nerves jangled.

Should he shout and make himself known, or try unobtrusively to make his way up to the house and assess the situation?

He shook his head again, and pulled himself together, striding forward almost angrily. *Don't be so soft. Don't be so damned soft!* He knew how to fight and the intruders were unlikely to be armed.

Or were they?

The dancing beam of light caught Herjólfur's attention again and this time it shone straight into his eyes. Startled, he stopped, more frightened than he dared admit even to himself, squinting into the blinding light.

'This is the police,' he called out, with as much authority as he could muster, the quaver in his voice belying his bravado. The wind swept away much of the strength he'd put into his words, but they must have been heard inside, behind those gaping window frames.

'This is the police,' he repeated. 'Who's in there?'

The light was directed at him a second time and he had an overwhelming feeling that he needed to move, to find some kind of refuge. But he hesitated, all the time aware that he was acting against his own instincts. A police officer is the one with authority, he reminded himself. He shouldn't let himself be rattled, feel the need to hide.

He took a step forward, closer to the house, his footsteps cautious. That was when he heard the shot, deafening and deadly.

2

It wasn't the first time that the crying of a child had woken Ari Thór. He looked at the clock and saw it was half-past five. He had gone to sleep early the previous night, after two days of battling a virulent bout of autumn flu, but it was still far too early to be awake.

Kristín was staying at home today. She had just returned to work at the hospital in Akureyri, but only part-time.

Everything to do with the baby was thoroughly organised, sometimes too organised, Ari Thór felt. Vegetables had to be organic, raised voices should never be heard in his vicinity, and when the little one crawled across the floor, it should, ideally, have just been mopped to spotless perfection.

The boy was approaching ten months, almost a year old. Ari Thór had suggested that Kristín should go back to work full-time; the hospital was waiting for her, struggling to cope with a shortage of doctors. *You can't keep the kid wrapped in cotton wool forever.*

And, if Ari Thór himself were to stay away from work any longer he'd risk losing his job. There had been talk of adding another police officer to the Siglufjördur force, but nothing had come of it. Cuts and savings were being made everywhere. A temporary officer had filled in while Ari Thór took his paternity leave, but had since returned to Reykjavík.

His role as a father was important to him, but it kept him busy, and was certainly a cause of tension every now and then between him and Kristín. Also, Ari Thór, being an only child, had little experience with children and initially struggled to get to grips with the basics. Then there was the issue of the boy's name. Ari Thór had waited until a few days after the birth to broach the subject. He knew it would a bone of contention and it was more a question of how serious the argument would be, rather than if there would be one at all. To begin with, in the rosy glow of the birth of his first child, he felt that the name wouldn't be all that important. Maybe it wasn't a good idea to stick to his guns, and upset the exquisite harmony that enveloped them. But his feelings surfaced again. It mattered. Ari Thór Arason was the clear choice, christening the child with the name of his own father who had died far too young.

'Then you'll be naming the child after yourself, as well,' Kristín had pointed out when the discussion resurfaced. 'What about my father? Is it right to leave either of them out?'

Ari decided not to make the obvious point his own father was no longer living, and that the name would be a well-deserved mark of respect. It was something that was deeply important to him, but he decided against inviting further dispute.

The result was that Kristín suggested christening the boy Stefnir: *one who leads the way.* A strong, vigorous name, but not a name from either his family or Kristín's. Ari Thór spent a day and a night thinking it over – a protest in itself, although he wasn't sure that the message had been clearly received.

Finally he agreed. He liked the name well enough and reckoned that the battle to name the child after his own father was as good as lost.

Kristín woke as Ari Thór shifted in bed. The child slept in an old cot in their bedroom and had started to cry vigorously. Ari Thór had bought it second-hand, having seen it advertised along with plenty of other stuff on the corkboard in the local Co-op. Up here business was done in the old-fashioned way and with no branch of Ikea anywhere to be found, furniture rarely found its way to the dump. The cot looked as good as new and he hadn't bothered to tell Kristín that it wasn't, as she probably would not have countenanced it with a newborn baby in the house.

Kristín stood up. 'Stay in bed,' she said. 'I don't want you giving Stefnir flu.'

He was thankful for the extra time in bed. He expected that he would need at least one more day off sick, which would mean another extra shift for Herjólfur.

He had made remarkably little contact with Herjólfur, his new superior. He was certainly an amiable and courteous character, as well as being a conscientious officer, but he came across as reserved. Disappointed at not being promoted, Ari Thór had to admit that he hadn't gone out of his way to make his new colleague feel welcome when he first arrived. This had probably coloured their subsequent relationship and Ari was sure that he would never be as close to Herjólfur as he had been to his predecessor, Tómas, who had gone on to a promotion with the Reykjavík force. Tómas had mentioned more than once, in an informal way, that one day Ari Thór might want to move south to Reykjavík and apply for a post there. The implication was that there would be a job to go to if he ever needed one.

Ari Thór was desperately keen to make the move and mentioned the idea to Kristín. Although she looked mildly interested, she reminded him that she had made a commitment to her own managers to stay in her job at the hospital in the nearby town of Akureyri for at least another year.

'Let's think about it next year,' she said with a smile. 'This small town life isn't so bad and all the sea air has to be good for Stefnir.'

Ari Thór sighed. *Why was she always so contrary, first hating the idea of Siglufjördur and now loving it?*

She had actually been unusually distant recently, and he couldn't understand quite why. It could hardly be baby blues; this coolness was something new and the boy was almost a year old now.

⊕

Ari Thór's mobile woke him. Kristín had already taken Stefnir downstairs, and the incessant ringing broke through the fragile tranquillity. He stretched for his phone with his eyes still closed. It was in its place on the nightstand, switched on day and night, whether he was on duty or not. There was no choice at a short-staffed police station in such a small community.

It would probably be Herjólfur calling to find out if he was well enough to return to work. Although Herjólfur wasn't a great talker, Ari Thór knew that he and his wife Helena were planning a trip south to Reykjavík. Herjólfur had once told him that they didn't really enjoy spending time outdoors and had never even been skiing, in spite of the excellent ski slopes just outside the town. This trip south, a trip to the theatre, Herjólfur had said, was important, and Ari Thór knew that he was expected to have shaken off the flu so they could go.

He answered without bothering to look at the screen and was startled to hear a female voice. This wasn't Herjólfur.

'Hello? Ari Thór?' There was a tremor in the voice that he didn't recognise. 'I hope I didn't wake you up.'

There was a moment's silence.

'Hello?' he said. 'Who is this?'

'It's Helena. Herjólfur's wife.'

Ari Thór sat up. He saw that it was almost six o'clock; he would have liked a little longer in bed.

'Hello,' he repeated, taken by surprise.

'I'm…' She hesitated. 'I'm looking for Herjólfur.'

'Looking for him?'

'He didn't come home after he went out last night. That's all I know. I was half-asleep. But he's not back and I couldn't get a reply when I called his phone.'

'He's not down at the station?' Ari Thór asked. 'I suppose he expected to be relieving me again today. I've had this miserable flu.'

'I called the station as well,' Helena said. 'No answer there.'

This was a strange situation.

'I'll try calling him and if I don't get an answer I'll take a look around the town and see if I can see the patrol car anywhere.'

'You haven't heard from him?' Helena asked, even though the answer was obvious.

'I'm afraid not. Leave it with me and I'll be in touch,' Ari said deci-sively, and ended the call. Punching in the number for Herjólfur's phone, he heard it ring without reply. It was tough having to be up and about in his condition, but there was no longer any choice in the matter.

Deciding against wearing his uniform, Ari Thór pulled on the clothes that he'd hung at the end of his bed, and made his way downstairs. Kristín was feeding Stefnir porridge, or doing her best anyway, as most of the food seemed to be on his face.

'I have to go out, and I'll need to borrow the car.'

There was only one car, Kristín's, which was used only for com-muting between Siglufjördur and Akureyri.

'Go out?' she asked with a look of surprise. 'You're ill, aren't you?'

'Yes, but Herjólfur has…' Ari Thór wasn't quite sure how to put it into words. 'He seems to have disappeared,' he said finally.

'Disappeared?' Kristín smiled. Ari Thór realised that it sounded incongruous for him to be leaving his sick bed to search for a grown man. 'You're telling me you've lost a whole policeman?'

The little boy gave him a smile. Everyone but Ari Thór seemed to be finding this amusing.

'I won't be long, sweetheart.'

⊕

Night was just turning into day in the little town.

Ari Thór drove to the police station to make sure that Herjólfur wasn't there, even checking inside, to be absolutely sure, but the station was empty. Herjólfur was nowhere to be seen.

There had to be some reasonable explanation, but, still groggy, Ari Thór struggled to see one. He drove slowly through the centre of town, then took a larger sweep through the side streets but there was no sign of the patrol car. Before going any further, Ari Thór decided that it would be worth taking a look at the only two roads leading out of the town, the road towards the old mountain tunnel, Strákar tunnel, and the road leading to the new Hédinsfjördur tunnel.

He knew he wasn't fit to drive, still half-asleep, sick and weak, and he had to do a double take when he saw the patrol car at the roadside near the Strákar tunnel entrance, next to the old house that had been empty and becoming steadily more dilapidated ever since he had moved to the town.

Growing increasingly uneasy, Ari Thór felt an overwhelming sense of foreboding – almost like a premonition. At that exact moment, he *knew* that something had happened to Herjólfur. With an adrenaline buzz providing the boost of energy he needed to sideline the flu for a while and think clearly, he pulled up behind the patrol car.

Bracing himself against the freezing rain, his eyes struggling to adjust in the darkness that preceded the dawn, he peered through the car windows, and then opened the doors of the patrol car to see if Herjólfur might be inside.

Empty.

His concern deepening, Ari Thór surveyed the landscape that surrounded him, the high mountain from which the road had literally been carved, and the sea on the other side. There was barely room for this single house there on the side of the road, on what was essentially a landfill site, and beyond it was a sheer and deadly drop into the cold, northern sea. There was no light from the house and no sign of his colleague. Making his way briskly towards the house, his jacket pulled tightly around him as the wind whipped the rain into a frenzy, he wondered if anyone would hear him if he called out. And then there was no need.

In the gravel a few yards away from the malevolent house lay a man in police uniform. He was completely still. Ari Thór shone his torch to be sure that it was Herjólfur, although he knew it could be no one else. The sight of the blood that was seeping into the puddles around the fallen man made him catch his breath, and he paused for a moment, struggling to believe what his own eyes were telling him, before bending down instinctively to search for signs of life. Fingers shaking, Ari Thór tried without success to find a pulse, and the thought occurred to him that he could be in danger himself.

Should he get away from the scene and call an ambulance from the car?

And then he felt it – he was certain he had found a faint pulse. Or was it just an illusion, hope defeating reality?

Pulling his phone from his pocket, he wiped the screen with the sleeve of his jacket, and called the emergency line, asking for an ambulance to be sent immediately, his voice high-pitched, odd to his own ears. It wasn't far to travel. The hospital was no distance away. He explained the situation in words as short and clear as he could manage.

'He's still alive?'

'I think so,' he replied quietly; and then, more loudly, and with determination, 'I think he is.'

There was no more that he could do. He was in no position to take any risks or assess the extent of Herjólfur's injuries.

He felt an instinctive urge to flee, to get himself to somewhere safer, but he couldn't bring himself to leave Herjólfur. He sat on the ground at his side, shivering uncontrollably. There was nobody to be seen and it was unusually dark over the fjord that morning. It was a gloomy time of year, with sunshine a rare visitor and in a few weeks the sun would disappear behind the mountains for two long months.

In the distance he saw lights and instinctively began rubbing Herjólfur's hand. 'They're coming,' he said in a low voice. 'It's going to be all right.' His words were sent spiralling away on the wind. It occurred to him that he was probably speaking to nobody but himself.

Just then an uncomfortable thought occurred to him, and he tried unsuccessfully to cast it from his mind, to stifle it before it grew any larger. *If Herjólfur could not return to duty, then the inspector's position was undoubtedly his.*

July 1982

At last they gave me a pencil and a notebook.

It's an old yellow pencil, badly sharpened, and an old notebook that someone has already used, the first few pages untidily ripped out. Had someone else already tried to put into words their difficulties and their helplessness, just as I'm doing? Maybe there were some pretty doodles there, the unchanging view of the back garden rendered in artistic form, if that could be done. Some things are so grey and cold that no amount of colour on a page could ever bring them to life.

I feel a little better now that I can scribble a few words on paper, but I can't explain exactly why. I've never taken any particular satisfaction from writing. It's only now that I have the feeling that this might save my life.

It probably doesn't even matter what I write here in this notebook. Maybe something of the background to my being here, my feelings and the monotonous existence in this place. Whatever it takes to maintain my sanity.

I've had practically no sleep for the last two nights. There's bright sunlight pretty much day and night, and these heavy curtains don't do much good. The sun sneaks its way past them to keep me awake. The brightness doesn't seem to bother my roommate and he's sound asleep all night long. He's just as quiet during the daylight hours, doesn't say a lot, the type who is sparing with words. In my innocence, I thought that I'd be happy with that, but on reflection I reckon there's a lot to be said for having someone to talk to.

I suppose I could have talked more to the nurse, but I don't really want to. She was the one who found the pencil and the notebook for me, that was good of her. But there's something about her that discourages me from coming closer. There's something about her eyes I don't like, something that tells me not to trust her. Not that I'm claiming my judgement is flawless right now, but I have to go by what my guts tell me.

It's a good while since the lights went out but I'm still sitting here writing in the half-dark. I pulled the curtain aside to let in a little light. It doesn't appear to disturb my roommate, any more than the scratching of my pencil does on these pages.

I can feel the weight of my own fatigue growing with every word that I write. At last. It's a familiar and long-awaited feeling. Maybe I can overcome the night-time brightness by simply embracing it.

No more now. Now I'm going to close the curtain and try to rest.

3

Gunnar Gunnarsson had pulled a good few strings to get this job.

A few months ago he had been appointed as the new mayor of the joint municipality of Siglufjördur and Ólafsfjördur, and so far he hadn't committed any serious howlers. He had cultivated an image of himself as a reliable, youthful and energetic official, and he came across well, dressed smartly, and on the job every day, devoting all his energy to running this small community. It went without saying that he had managed to upset a few of the vested interests of the local big shots, but that was only to be expected. The financial wellbeing of individuals and companies don't always coincide with those of the community, and planning issues often became battlegrounds.

Through the innocent eyes of his own children, Gunnar had seen that there are clear dividing lines between good and evil, right and wrong. People are either bad or good. Then as the years pass, those lines become steadily less clear.

On a fundamental level, he was a good guy, although there probably was a skeleton or two rattling at the back of his closet. That phone call had shaken him badly, woken him out of a daze, and now he knew that he would have to shape up.

He had a few extenuating circumstances. Times were hard. His wife had moved to Norway and taken their two children with her. They weren't divorced. Divorce was a word they avoided, but every day that passed brought that possibility closer. His wife was a doctor and had been given the opportunity to take up a post at a large Oslo hospital. At the outset, Gunnar had moved with the rest of the family, but he struggled to find work, and was disappointed that his BA in political science from an Icelandic university didn't open many doors in Norway. In spite of his wife's encouragement, he couldn't face being a house-husband, even though she reminded him that her salary in those precious Norwegian kroner was easily enough to keep them and the children afloat.

Gunnar was awake very early that morning, tired after a difficult night. Some nights, sleep became nothing more than a fleeting, elusive commodity, dipping in and out of consciousness, which was far from restful. But he had had more than one sleepless night without his colleagues at the municipal offices noticing. Of course, he couldn't hide anything from Elín any more than he usually could, but that wouldn't be a problem.

Elín followed him like a shadow. They had studied together and then taken their first steps together in journalism. They were the closest of friends and this was a friendship that had not proved to have a positive effect on his marriage. The frown on his wife's face whenever Elín's name was mentioned bore witness to the lack of trust, as if it was assumed that he was in love with Elín and they were sleeping together. He had to admit, solely to himself and not to anyone else, that she was pretty magnificent, both smart and charming, but so far he had resisted any temptation. It had never occurred to him that she wouldn't be available if he were to show an interest, and over the years he reckoned that he had seen plenty of clues to suggest that she might. Self-confidence was something he had never lacked.

Now his marriage was in the worst shape it had ever been. Sixteen hundred kilometres and a whole ocean separated him from his wife, and relations had been difficult, with both of them dissatisfied and easily irritated. Under these circumstances he could hardly be expected to be completely faithful, at least not in physical terms. And it was a fortunate coincidence that Elín happened to be single these days.

He had offered her the deputy mayor's post the moment the news had come through that the mayor's job was his. First he had to give notice to the existing deputy, and Gunnar was happy to take on that battle, as getting rid of someone with close links to the previous majority on the council suited the new majority. He had no intention of moving north alone with no allies of his own to back him up and Elín fitted the bill perfectly.

The appointment to mayor of such a small town wasn't exactly his dream job, but it would do. It came with power and a decent salary, plus experience that would be useful later on. He had taken the initiative and applied for the post when an old friend had been elected to the council as part of the majority in power. Gunnar contacted him and found that the intention was to employ a professional manager, so Gunnar's appointment suited them both. Gunnar found himself with a job that plenty of people had wanted and his friend on the council found himself with a mayor he could trust and support behind the scenes.

A little icing had been needed on the cake to seal the appointment. During Gunnar's six months in Oslo he had applied for an unpaid internship at a Norwegian ministry. His application had been received favourably, although he had the feeling that this was no great achievement as they probably accepted anyone who might be prepared to work for nothing. He was given study facilities at a ministry in the centre of Oslo, among students who were all much younger than he was. The work was far from exciting and the fact that his command of Norwegian wasn't as good as he had made out in his application didn't help make his time there any easier. But when it came to putting together a CV for his application for the mayor's post, his internship became a job and one month became an unspecified period under the loose heading 'consultation on parliamentary administration' that had found its way into the text. This experience in Norway clearly had the desired effect when it came to the decision of who should be the lucky applicant, or so Gunnar heard later.

He would never have chosen Siglufjördur if a larger municipality had been available. His family wasn't from the north and he had virtually no personal links to the district, although the fact that he was untainted by local tradition, gossip, small-town politics and old feuds was a strong point in his favour.

He was living in rented property in Siglufjördur, a roomy detached house in the newer part of the town, in the shadow of the town's avalanche defences. So far he hadn't seen any huge weight of winter snow, but these imposing defensive walls still gave him a feeling of security. Plenty of people had told him how relaxing it must be to have moved to such a close-knit coastal community with the mountains and the sea as his neighbours. Normally he just smiled his agreement, while inside he failed to understand what was so enchanting about loneliness, isolation and cold.

He sat naked at the kitchen table, half asleep and drinking black coffee as he stared out of the window. More wind and pouring rain was the only description that fitted the morning's weather. There was no way to give it a slightly more romantic edge, even here in this bucolic paradise. These were the days when he had no desire to leave the house. There was no way he was staying here for long; the four years between one council election and the next would be about right and then he'd be able to nail down a better job, preferably somewhere closer to the city and ideally somewhere abroad. But that meant keeping his nose clean and making a decent job of things while he was here. Not that there was much he could mess up in a town like this, surely? No, he told himself. That wasn't where the minefields were. It was his personal life that he needed to take care of; he absolutely could not destroy this fragile success that he had achieved, and there were a few secrets that must never see the light of day. Sometimes he could be his own worst enemy.

Then that phone call from the police inspector came to mind. He was just the kind of miserable character who could wreck everything for him.

4

Ari Thór stood in the corridor of the hospital.

Herjólfur had been hit by a shotgun blast at short range. The doctor said it was practically a miracle that he had survived. It was impossible to believe that Herjólfur had been shot on duty; that kind of thing never happened, particularly not in such a close community. But it could hardly have been an accident. There was no hunting in that area and any hunter would have called in to let the authorities know if something had gone wrong. This was unreal, disturbing. The media spotlight would undoubtedly shine on the case and that would make the investigation even more complex.

Ari Thór realised immediately, or at least expected, that someone from outside would have to be brought in to investigate. He was aware that the victim's subordinate was hardly the best person to handle such a case. An early-morning call to the chief of police in Akureyri had confirmed this.

'You're right,' he had said. 'We'll need to appoint someone else to lead this, but I want you to be a part of the investigation, Ari Thór.'

Ari Thór had his own ideas about who would be best suited to deal with the case and took the liberty of putting forward a suggestion.

A police officer from a neighbouring town had been called in to keep watch at the crime scene until reinforcements could arrive.

Herjólfur wasn't dead. At least not yet. Ari Thór searched the doctor's face as he explained the severity of the injuries. An emergency medical flight to Reykjavík had been requested.

The chief of police in Akureyri had given Ari Thór an important assignment to carry out; a job he was dreading. He stood indecisively in the hospital corridor, telling himself that he should wait for more news of Herjólfur's condition, but deep down he knew that he couldn't put this off any longer. Tales would find their way around the town quickly enough and he must not allow Herjólfur's wife to hear dreadful gossip first.

He wondered about contacting his friend, the Reverend Eggert, the local priest. He almost had the phone in his hand when he changed his mind. Herjólfur was still alive and the priest's presence would send every kind of wrong message to the family.

As he left the hospital the town was just starting to come to life, although the weather was so foul that nobody was likely to be in a hurry to leave home. The all-too-familiar northerly wind was blowing, bitterly cold, something Ari Thór would probably never get used to, with heavy rain to add to the discomfort. Just a few degrees colder and this would have been the recipe for a blizzard.

Ari Thór was almost ashamed that he knew so little about Herjól-fur's family. He remembered his wife's name, Helena, but hadn't met her. This morning was the first time he had spoken to her, and under such strange circumstances. How many children did Herjólfur have? He *had* mentioned children, but Ari Thór had no idea if there were two of them or more, or what their ages might be. He guessed they might be teenagers. Herjólfur wasn't the talkative type but Ari Thór had to admit that he could have made a better effort to get to know him. He knew it wasn't Herjólfur's fault that the promotion hadn't come his way. But Ari Thór had somehow decided, unconsciously rather than deliberately, to keep his dealings with him formal and professional; never discourteous, but equally, not too friendly.

He hesitated by the front door, waiting for a moment before ringing the doorbell. The rain was hammering down with even greater force and the storm had gathered strength. It was on days like this that the undisputed beauty of the fjord and the mountains gave way to forces of nature, and the town looked bleak and very, very wet.

Suddenly he felt overwhelmed and was transported back fifteen years to another wet, windy day. A little boy, Ari Thór had returned

home from school to find a police car in the drive. He had stood
and stared at it in the rain, buying himself time, just as he was doing
now. The thought had crossed his mind that the police would be
bringing him bad news, and he had been right about that. There
were two officers, one young and quiet, the other older and clearly
the man with experience, with a deep voice and a serious expression
on his face, a pair who could just as easily have been Ari Thór and
Tómas. Already soaked by the rain, Ari Thór hadn't been able to hold
back the tears.

The memories came back to him and flashed past like a film,
frame after frame, and he recalled it all with uncomfortable clarity.

Sometimes it was better just to forget.

He had been sitting on the sofa when he was given the news. Ari
Thór had been expecting something like this, ever since his father
had disappeared without trace, but what he heard next confused and
stunned him. Not his father. His mother. His mother had lost her
life in a car crash. The shock was indescribable, and everything he
knew and was changed in a flash. Still a child at thirteen years old,
he had grown up in a matter of moments. From that point on, he
had been an orphan. It was an event, a defining moment, that he was
still getting over.

Now, once again, he was soaked through in the punishing wind
and rain, but this time playing a different role. He was the bearer of
bad news, and once he had rung the doorbell, there would be no way
back. Their world wouldn't be the same again.

⊕

The young man who answered the door was unmistakably Herjólfur's son. Tall, and with a determined countenance, he looked to
be around twenty and certainly resembled his father. As if he knew
what was coming, he wordlessly gestured Ari Thór inside, his expression dark and serious.

The living room was oddly off-putting, with mismatched furniture that gave it a cold and impersonal feel. *A house rather than a home.* The only item with life in it was an old, black piano that looked well used, cherished.

A middle-aged woman who could only be Helena, Herjólfur's wife, sat on a white leather sofa, its newness and incongruity suggesting a hasty, perhaps thoughtless purchase. She did not stand up as Ari Thór came into the room. She sat still, a thick red blanket over her legs, and looked at him with empty eyes.

Ari Thór was silent as he wrestled with the right words, aware of the impact they would have, remembering being in a similar situation himself. His concentration betrayed him; he longed to be anywhere but here, forced to bring this family such terrible news. Finally he blurted, 'Herjólfur is in hospital … It looks serious. He seems to have been…' He paused, struggling to find a compassionate way to express the reality of the situation. 'Shot by accident.'

Helena's face did not change. Ari Thór looked at the son, who stood stock still, and then sat wordless by his mother, grasping her hand tightly. A spasm of pain flashed across her face as she twisted herself on the sofa to face him, moving one leg awkwardly beneath the red blanket.

Ari Thór waited in the overwhelming silence, cleared his throat and continued. 'He hasn't regained consciousness and I expect he'll be taken to Reykjavík on an emergency medical flight, probably within minutes. They had one ready at Akureyri and it's probably landed here by now.' He was silent for a few seconds. 'Do you want me to find out if you can go with him?' he added.

Helena shook her head. 'I don't think I can,' she said at last. She looked at her son. 'You have to call your sister.'

Two children, then. Ari Thór waited but neither Helena nor her son said anything. It seemed like they wanted him to leave.

He was about to make his excuses when she spoke suddenly. 'By accident?' she asked.

'He appears to have been injured in a firearms incident,' he said. 'A shotgun at short range.'

'And who shot him?' she asked, her gaze still distant.

'That isn't clear at the moment but we'll find him. Don't you worry.'

She posed another question in a low voice. 'Where did this happen?'

'Outside an old house out by the tunnel, the Strákar tunnel.'

'Old house?' She looked at him in disbelief.

'Yes, an abandoned house.'

'That old place?' she asked haltingly. 'What on earth was he doing out there?'

Ari Thór was silent for a few seconds before he answered. *If only I knew*, he thought.

'That's what we're trying to establish,' he said, as decisively as he could. He was starting to feel deeply uncomfortable; the memory of the two police officers telling him of his mother's death was still raw, as was his recollection of longing to be rid of them as quickly as possible so he could deal with his bereavement in solitude. 'I know this must be extremely difficult for you,' he said to fill the silence. 'Please get in touch if there's anything I can help with … and I'll let you know the moment there's anything new to report.'

Helena stared at him sorrowfully, but said nothing. Willowy slim, her face etched with strong lines and framed by raven-black hair, she was arresting even in her grief. This was someone it would be difficult to forget; someone Ari Thór would definitely always remember.

'I can ask the priest to stop by and see you later,' he said. 'He can help you deal with things,' he added, against his own instincts. Nobody had made the loss of his mother easier, still less the disappearance of his father, not the priest nor anyone else. Any belief in a higher power had definitely been lost that rainy day when he had learned of his mother's fate.

Now Herjólfur's son spoke for the first time, his eyes not quite meeting Ari Thór's. 'Thank you. It's appreciated. But we're not particularly religious.'

Ari Thór nodded and allowed himself a thin smile.

He didn't say any formal goodbyes, letting himself disappear quietly. No one followed him to the door. He closed it carefully behind him and walked briskly to the car, willing himself not to break into a run.

Then he heard the door open and someone calling quietly. 'Hey, Ari Thór…'

He turned to see Herjólfur's son frowning in the doorway, waiting for him to retrace his steps.

He extended a hand. 'I'm sorry … I'm Herjólfur's son, and my name's Herjólfur, too.'

Ari Thór shook the outstretched hand. He was about to say 'my condolences' but stopped himself just in time. That would have been too much, as if admitting that there was no hope.

'It's terrible. I know how you feel,' he said instead.

The boy's expression made it plain that he doubted Ari Thór could understand how he felt.

'I think I know what Dad was doing up there,' he said.

'Really?' Ari Thór asked, with surprise and interest.

'He told me about it the other day, said it was to do with a case he's been working on. You probably know all about it…'

This was news to Ari Thór. 'Well…' he said doubtfully, not wanting to admit that there was clearly something that Herjólfur had not trusted him enough to tell him. He decided to let silence work for him and prompt a further answer.

'It was a dope case,' the younger Herjólfur said at last.

'Drugs?'

'Yes, people meet there to sell dope, you know…'

'Yes, I see.'

'Dad thought I might be able to help him, wanted to know if any of the kids at school knew anything about it. I'm at college here, graduating in the spring.'

Ari Thór waited.

'But I didn't know anything. People aren't going to trust a cop's son with that kind of information.'

'No, I understand,' Ari Thór said.

'There's something … something sensitive about this case, Dad reckoned,' the younger Herjólfur added.

'Sensitive? What do you mean by that?' Ari Thór asked, unnecessarily sharply.

'Some political connection, or so I understood.'

Ari Thór waited for Herjólfur to continue, but he appeared to have no more to say.

'He didn't explain any further than that?' Ari Thór asked eventually.

'No, unfortunately not.' Herjólfur hung his head.

Ari Thór thanked him for the information, said his goodbyes and walked back to the car. He looked over his shoulder quickly before he got in. The younger Herjólfur had gone and the door of the big house had shut behind him. The sky continued to weep, and the wind continued her howling. Ari Thór was thankful to be out of the house with that particular job behind him, and with the sorrow at arm's length, for the moment.

He was, however, painfully aware that this was only the beginning.

It's still night. I managed to sleep a little.

I came here to the hospital late one evening, and all I really wanted to do was to go back home, curl up in bed and sleep. Of course I could have tried to refuse being admitted, but Dad had already made up his mind, there was no shifting him, and he's not a man who takes no for an answer.

That evening is a blur, although there are a few things that I remember. The doctor on duty, Helgi. He was friendly but firm and agreed that I should come here. Dad was convincing, as always, and I just mumbled a series of nothings under my breath.

He was a young man, that doctor, maybe fifteen or so years older than me. I'd guess that would make him thirty-five. He had a deep voice, a convincing voice.

How long am I supposed to be here? I asked.

He should have said: until you want to leave. That would have been the right answer.

As long as you need to, was what he said, with a look on his face that said he was better than me, so much better than me. It was as if any decision had been taken out of my hands, and that's the way I still feel, like a sleepwalker, bereft of will, imprisoned in my own body.

Then they took a blood test.

I can see from the window that I'm on the first floor. I have a recollection of how I got up here. I was taken along a long corridor, painfully long, to my mind. The walls were reminiscent of jagged lava, rough; no, they were positively sharp. They'd be dangerous if you were to catch yourself against them. It sounds like the ravings of a disturbed mind, but that's the way it was. I remember clearly thinking at the time that if I still, really and genuinely, want to hurt myself, then all I'd need to do is to run into those damned walls. I never did it. Maybe because I was too tired, too apathetic, too frightened. Maybe because I had never actually intended to finish myself off. A few shallow cuts in the inside of one arm, *a half-hearted suicide attempt, that was enough for Dad to panic and for Mum to come close to a nervous breakdown.*

Even though I don't want to be here, I'm determined to tough it out. Maybe all this will do me some good. It's the best you can expect, considering what happened, Dad said. That may well be right, but deep inside I fear that the opposite could be true.

5

'You know what? This is the first time I've been back to Siglufjördur since we sold the house,' Tómas said, trying to make himself comfortable in a chair that hadn't been designed for comfort. He had responded quickly and arrived that afternoon. They sat in the police station's kitchen, just as they had in the old days. Ari Thór felt an unexpected twinge of regret. Although he had applied energetically for the inspector's post when Tómas moved to Reykjavík, he would still have preferred things to have remained as they had been. He would have liked at least a few years more of working with Tómas. They got on well together; Tómas was a patient character and a good teacher, although he could be more than a little stubborn on occasion. As Tómas's replacement, Herjólfur hadn't been an improvement.

'I went past our old place on the way here,' Tómas said, in the awkwardly ponderous way he sometimes adopted. 'That was a strange feeling, I can tell you. That doctor who bought the place has made himself at home. New curtains in all the windows, when the ones we had left him were perfectly good. And he's extended the decking and built a windbreak – looks like he's even put in a hot tub there. A hot tub!' He shook his head and sighed. 'He's rooted out all the plants and shrubs.'

Ari Thór smiled for the first time that day. He had managed to get home after talking to the family, hoping to rest for a while, but that hadn't happened. The flu still had him in its grip, although he was just managing to keep it at bay.

'You were quick getting here,' Ari Thór said. It was getting on for three o'clock. Herjólfur had been flown south; his prospects of recovery were still unclear, and he had not regained consciousness. The incident had already attracted much media interest even though a formal press conference had not yet been held. An armed attack on a police officer was certainly big news, particularly in a small community like this one.

'Yes, they called me at some ungodly hour,' Tómas said. 'I gather you suggested me.'

'I think the chief had been thinking along the same lines,' Ari Thór protested. 'There aren't many police officers who know Siglufjördur as well as you do, which makes you the ideal man for this kind of assignment,' he added and immediately regretted using the word. It seemed wrong to be talking about an assignment under the present circumstances.

Tómas looked away, avoiding Ari Thór's eyes.

'I take it you'll be helping me with the investigation?' he asked. 'That shouldn't be an issue, as long as it's formally in my hands. But it looks to me that you're not in the best of health?' he spoke more softly, with an almost fatherly tone.

'Well, I'm supposed to be on sick leave today, but of course I'm ready to do what I can,' Ari Thór replied. 'It's just the two of us?'

'Not a chance. The technical team is on the way to the crime scene and they'll search every square inch of that damned house. Then there are two lads we can have, one from Ólafsfjördur and one from Akureyri, if we need them. They'll start by making house-to-house enquiries in the area to find out if anyone heard a shot or noticed any unusual movements … any unfamiliar cars about. You know. I'm not hopeful, but you can never tell.'

Tómas stood up, ready to leave. He looked out of the window for a while. The rain had stopped but the town still looked grey and drab. The wonderful glow that normally bathed the town in the summer was now gone, but the picture-perfect charm of a snowy winter hadn't yet arrived; it was as if Siglufjördur was caught in a limbo between two worlds at this time of year, and it certainly wasn't Ari Thór's favourite season.

'So,' Tómas said at last and turned around. 'Where shall we start?'
Ari Thór hesitated. It was a question he hadn't expected.

'The weapon,' he said at last. 'Where did the weapon come from?'

'Quite right,' Tómas said. 'We'll get a ballistics report from Reykjavík and hopefully they'll be able to tell us what type of shotgun
was used. If the weapon is legally registered then it shouldn't be a
problem to track down the owner sooner or later.'

'There's no guarantee that the shotgun is a registered weapon,
even though it should be,' Ari Thór said, and related his earlier conversation with Herjólfur's son.

'Dope, you reckon?' Tómas said thoughtfully. 'Drugs have never
been that much of a problem in Siglufjördur, although I gather it's
been more of a problem since the new tunnel was built, bringing the
place closer to the main roads. For better or worse.'

'And this political angle. Any idea what that might be?' Ari asked.

'No, there's nothing that springs to mind. There aren't that many
politicians around here, just a few town councillors who aren't
exactly the type to be involved with drugs. Some of them are kids I
knew when they were still in nappies.' Tómas smiled broadly.

Ari Thór knew that there was no need to take Tómas too seriously
when he referred to 'kids'.

'There are some politicians from Reykjavík who have summer
houses here,' Ari Thór said thoughtfully.

'Don't even mention that. It makes me want to weep,' Tómas said.
He had never been shy of sharing his robust views on Siglufjördur
turning into a summer-house district. The local property market
was thriving, certainly doing better than it had around the turn of
the century when the declining fishing industry had seen the town
become less prosperous. Since then, local people who had moved
away had been buying houses in the town and doing them up as
summer homes. Skiing enthusiasts had been doing much the same,
as the Skardsdalur ski slopes inside the town limits were particularly
popular.

Ari Thór remained puzzled by the attraction of skiing. He had borrowed skis a few times and tried out the slopes after moving north, but it seemed to him as if the skis were controlling him rather than the other way around. He guessed that wasn't the way it was supposed to be. He mentally reprimanded himself for allowing his thoughts to wander at such a critical time.

Tómas continued, apparently not noticing his deputy's poor concentration, 'It wouldn't do any harm if something as unpleasant as a shooting could be blamed on some outsider. But we shouldn't be too hopeful…'

Tómas still hadn't sat down. He seemed to think better on his feet.

'We still don't know who Herjólfur talked to last night,' he went on. 'His phone is locked, but we'll hopefully be able to sort that out later today.'

'I've been through his duty records and there's nothing there that jumps out as being unusual,' Ari Thór said. 'We can try and get into his email to see if there is anything there.'

'Absolutely,' Tómas sighed. 'It's a damned nightmare. A damned nightmare! I simply cannot remember a police officer *ever* being injured in a firearms attack in this country. You can imagine the turmoil this is causing in Reykjavík. They're in a blind panic at headquarters, every one of them. This is something that just shouldn't happen!'

'No…' Ari Thór said thoughtfully, an unsettling idea striking him as he uttered the words, 'It could have been me.'

Tómas frowned and was quiet for a moment.

'It's possible.'

'More than possible,' Ari Thór said sharply. '*I* should have been on duty last night. This bloody flu saved my life.'

'It's possible,' Tómas repeated patiently. 'Of course we can't rule out that Herjólfur was the target.'

'No, I can't imagine that,' Ari Thór said firmly, still upset at the thought that he could have been there in Herjólfur's place, and Kristín in Helena's position.

That would have left little Stefnir without a father and Ari Thór could hardly bring himself to think it through any further.

'Who could have wanted him dead? It's not as if we made a point of letting people know that he was on duty instead of me.'

'Whatever happens,' Tómas said, with rising impatience. 'We need to get to know Herjólfur better. Talk to his wife when she's had a chance to, to collect herself, as much as she can, anyhow. Had he crossed swords with anyone in the town? Had he received any threats?'

'His wife would have mentioned it,' Ari Thór said.

'You're sure? I doubt she was that talkative after receiving news like that.'

'No, she wasn't,' Ari Thór admitted. 'She didn't say a lot and seemed to be in shock.'

'We'll pay her a visit tomorrow. I hear she's been unwell,' Tómas added.

'Unwell? What's wrong with her?'

'I'm not sure. I know that Herjólfur had finished a year's leave when he got the promotion and the posting here. He was granted extended leave to look after his wife.'

'A year off? That's quite something. He really made sacrifices for her then.'

'Hmm. I don't know about that,' Tómas said, and dropped his voice as if Herjólfur was listening in around the corner of the kitchen. 'He was on full pay the whole time.'

'Full pay? That's not bad at all. We're clearly members of a pretty decent union.'

'I'm not sure the union had anything to do with the decision. He's well connected. His father was a legend in his own lifetime, a copper of the old school, high-ranking and plenty of influence. He was a shrewd one. I remember meeting him once, a proper tough character. He's dead now, the old man. But we can say that Herjólfur had blue blood in his veins, royalty within the force, you understand?'

'That's why he got the job and I didn't?'

'More than likely.'

Ari Thór was silent.

'Then there's something else ... that old house by the tunnel,' Tómas began. 'That place has a weird history. Twin brothers lived there around the middle of the century, inherited the house from their parents. One night around 1960, one of the twins was found dead at the back of the house, and it looked as if he had fallen off the balcony. There was talk that there had been drinking there the night before, as the twins had had a visitor, but as far as I know, nobody ever found out what really happened. Some people believed that the surviving brother was responsible, that he lost his wits. He changed completely after the incident, became something of a recluse. The matter was allowed to drop, as some awkward cases were at that time. Some said that the man had simply fallen. That's how I heard it, anyway...'

'You don't think there's some connection there?' Ari Thór asked curiously.

'I doubt it. But we'll have to be open to every possibility.'

Ari Thór stood up too quickly. He still wasn't well. His head spun and he felt nauseous, but he forced himself past it. Drops of sweat formed on his forehead.

'Are you sure you're up for this?' Tómas looked ready to send Ari Thór home to bed.

'Of course. I'm all right.'

His voice was determined, but still didn't sound convincing.

'Fair enough. We'd best be on our way. I reckon we should start with Addi Gunna. He's bound to be at home.'

'Addi Gunn? Who's that?'

'Addi Gunna, not Addi Gunn. His mother's name was Gunna and the moniker comes from her. His father was some Reykjavík deadbeat. Gunna was Siglufjördur born and bred, came from a good family up here, but Addi, he's had a few ups and downs in life.'

'I've never heard of him.'

Now they were outside the police station.

Tómas sat in the car. 'No surprise, as you're still something of a newcomer. Siglufjördur people know Addi Gunna. He was for a long time, and may well still be, the only person in town who has done time for handling dope, more than likely several times. He moved north about ten, fifteen years ago when his mother died and he's been keeping his nose clean ever since, at least on the surface. I always kept an eye on him while I was up here. It wouldn't surprise me if he is still in the business even though he's pushing sixty. Maybe he's just more discreet than he used to be.'

'You never mentioned him to me before you left,' Ari Thór said, almost accusingly. 'You could have said something.'

'Well ... somehow I didn't feel it was right to be asking you to keep tabs on the old boy. And as it happens, we are related, second cousins.'

Ari Thór looked at Tómas in silence. Things were becoming more complicated by the moment, and suddenly Ari Thór felt like the outsider again, the same feeling he'd had when he first moved to town. A stranger in a place where everyone was connected and nobody could be trusted completely.

6

'Tómas. Good to see you, cousin.'

They shook hands.

'I was expecting to see you. Heard the midday news on the radio,' he said, his voice rasping and assertive.

'This is…' Tómas said, before he was interrupted.

'Ari Thór Arason. I know,' Addi said, finishing his sentence for him.

'Have we met?' Ari Thór asked, immediately on the defensive. He didn't recall having encountered this man before, and he was a figure he could hardly have forgotten. He looked closer to seventy than sixty, tall and rangy, with a narrow face, his veins and bones prominent, eyes large and protruding from his face. He was wearing a thick seaman's jersey, and holding a cigarette that smouldered between his fingers, a long, thin brand that had been fashionable several decades earlier.

'Don't think so,' he drawled in reply. 'But don't get upset, my boy, everyone in town knows who you are. How's Kristín?' Addi grinned, baring yellow teeth.

'You're not going to ask us in?' Tómas managed to ask, before Ari Thór had a chance to respond to such an over-familiar question. He did his best to stay calm, to stem the anger welling up inside him. How could this criminal dare to ask about Kristín? Was this some kind of subtle threat?

'In you go.'

The flat was reasonably tidy, apart from the brimming ashtrays on practically every surface. The stench of tobacco was almost overwhelming. Ari Thór was immediately reminded of his late grandmother's flat, where he'd been brought up after the deaths of his parents. The old lady had been strongly against both tobacco and alcohol, so there had been no ashtrays or the lingering smell of stale smoke, but something about the place sparked his memory. The living room had presumably been furnished by Addi's mother, someone of the same generation as Ari Thór's grandmother. There was no indication that Addi had made any attempt to put his own stamp on the place after his mother had died, living instead in her shadow.

'You want to sit down?' he said gruffly, drawing on his cigarette.

'Thanks but no thanks,' Tómas said. 'We're in a hurry.'

Ari Thór kept quiet, standing next to Tómas, and feeling his hostility growing by the minute, increasing with every second that passed.

'I reckon you know, or at least you can guess, which police officer was attacked,' Tómas continued. Herjólfur's name still had not been released to the media.

'Of course. You didn't come here to tell me that.'

Addi sat down in an old wine-red armchair.

'You know the house, where it took place?'

'Should I know it?' Addi asked, an almost playful tone to his voice.

'The old place up by...'

'Yeah, yeah. I know,' Addi interrupted.

'We suspect that Herjólfur was investigating some narcotics business going on there,' Tómas said formally. 'Know anything about it?'

'You've got a nerve, cousin. Asking me if I'm selling dope and shooting bloody coppers.'

'Come on, Addi,' Tómas snapped.

'One damned conviction and you're a criminal for ever more.'

'More than one conviction,' Tómas said.

'And what the hell am I supposed to say? Give you some bullshit? Drop my mates in it?'

'Someone tried to murder a police officer,' Tómas said firmly. 'I'm not accusing you of having anything to do with it, but if you know anything about this, it's as well to say so. Trying to protect whoever was behind this isn't going to help anyone. You can expect this crime to be dealt with rigorously, just so you know.'

Addi puffed his cigarette in silence.

'I'm just an old guy. You know that, Tómas, and you know I wouldn't shoot anyone, not even a cop...' he said, and his voice faded away.

'Do you know who could have done it?'

'Who knows? Eh? I'm not responsible for all the local dope heads.'

'Has the building been used for that kind of activity?'

'Could have been.'

'Yes or no?'

'Yeah, yeah. As far as I know. OK?'

'What went on there?'

'Just business. People stash gear there, someone else picks it up. Understand? It was a good place to choose, since you guys can't be bothered to drive out of town any more. That's right, isn't it?'

Tómas left the question hanging unanswered. Ari Thór knew that there was truth behind what the man was telling them, and he seemed convincing.

'You have anything to do with these people? These guys and their ... business?'

'No, cousin. This...' He pointed his cigarette towards Tómas. 'This is the closest I've come to any dope since I moved back home.'

'Was anyone there that night?'

Ari Thór was still taking care to keep quiet.

'I wouldn't know,' Addi muttered. 'But it's not as if I know everything that goes on around here.'

'Who else would it be worth speaking to? Someone who's been involved with the, you know, the practical side of the business recently?'

Addi laughed.

'Cousin Tómas,' he said. 'I don't have a clue.'

'Don't let the old boy upset you,' Tómas said when they had left Addi and were back in the car. 'He's always been like that.'

Ari Thór's voice was a little shaky when he spoke. 'No chance of that.'

Addi's innocent mention of Kristín's name had infuriated him. If there was one thing Ari Thór was afraid of, it was his own temper, especially if there was even a hint of threat towards his family. He hoped that he had read too much into Addi's comments, but couldn't stop himself from fearing the worst.

I've just had breakfast, or what they call breakfast.

Rye bread with butter and some fruit, served on the usual plastic trays. I wasn't even going to bother going to the canteen, but the nurse made me go.

It'll do you good, she said.

These days there seem to be plenty of things that will do me good.

I let her have her way. Couldn't be bothered to argue with her. The first morning I got breakfast in bed, but that's not on offer any longer.

It seems I don't try hard enough to mix with the others, with the other … well … patients. I've never been exactly shy, but I don't care to get to know them. I don't want to be part of the group, be one of them. I don't belong here. The one I've talked to the most is the nurse, even though I don't like her.

I have never been shy, but there has always been a fear, tucked away at the back of my mind. Maybe it's that fear that's starting to surface now, fighting its way out. There has always been a timidity in me, for as far back as I can remember. There are, of course, reasons for it, more than one, I'm sure.

7

Kristín was exhausted. The little boy was finally asleep, his afternoon nap taking place later than usual. Everything was happening at once. After the call-out in the middle of the night, Ari Thór had come home quickly to give her the terrible news. It was such a shock, and so difficult to take in that she found it hard to believe.

Her first reaction was to offer to help.

'Is there anything I can do? I can go up to the hospital now if the babysitter's free,' she said, every inch the doctor ready for an emergency.

'Thanks, but I think he'll be sent south to Reykjavík as soon as possible. He may have gone already.'

She wanted to ask him about the victim's injuries, to try and assess his chances of survival, but couldn't bring herself to delve into the details of this particular tragedy.

She realised immediately that Ari Thór was the one who should have been on duty, not Herjólfur. But she carefully said nothing, seeing that he was already badly shaken.

The thought that she could have lost him set her conscience nagging at her, and not least in connection with the new doctor who had recently joined the staff at the hospital in Akureyri. He was seven years older than she was, divorced and recently moved back to Iceland from Sweden, where he had studied and worked. He was tall and elegant, extremely clever, as well as patient and thoughtful; in some ways similar to Ari Thór and in other ways his opposite. Ari Thór could sometimes be awkwardly reckless and self-absorbed, sharp-tongued and prone to dark moods. He remained caught up in the past, having never properly come to terms with the loss of his parents, and for some reason these wounds refused to heal. He was equally caught up in present problems, destined, it seemed, to be stuck in a rut. Not getting the promotion to inspector had been a bitter disappointment and he wasn't sure whether to stay or leave, so Kristín had taken the decision for them both. She liked Siglufjördur and living there while working at the hospital in Akureyri suited her. It wasn't far now that the new tunnel was open.

It was such a lovely town, she had to admit, despite her earlier scepticism. She revelled in the long, bright days of summer, the wonderful scent of the sea, the cold but utterly fresh air that filled her with renewed energy every day, even in winter. She actually even liked the rain and the wind, like today; it made her feel alive. To be honest, she probably even preferred the winter months to the brief summer, the warmth of the darkness that engulfed the town – and also the fact that now, with the new tunnel, she could drive into neighbouring Hédinsfjördur, an abandoned fjord, with relative ease. In winter, she could enjoy almost total darkness there, on fine nights looking up to the astonishingly clear, starlit skies and, when she was lucky, the mesmerising northern lights. But Siglufjördur wasn't where she was going to stay and she had pretty much made up her mind to continue her studies abroad in two or three years, once the boy was a little older.

The question was whether or not Ari Thór would be going with them; and whether or not she *wanted* him to go with them. The other question was whether a long, hard look would find any real future in this relationship. She had pushed all these questions to the back of her mind for a long time now, with the same doubts lurking on the edges of her consciousness, far enough away to be ignored. That is, until this doctor had appeared from Sweden. Kristín had spent a lot of time working with him once her maternity leave had come to an end and she had begun shifts at the hospital on a part-time basis. They had formed an immediate friendship. In fact, it was disturbing just how well they got on together. They seemed to have interests and opinions that dovetailed neatly. They went to lunch together and took their coffee breaks at the same time and, although neither of them overstepped any marks, she felt comfortable with this man. Strictly speaking, no written or unwritten relationship rules had been broken, nothing had happened she needed to be ashamed of, but she knew she was standing on the edge of a precipice and it wasn't somewhere she could stay for long.

She liked this guy, the doctor, there was no question about that. But was she in love with him? Hardly. But was she in love with Ari Thór? Or had it just been a deep-seated affection for him that had resulted in the birth of their wonderful boy? And could she do this to her son, break up the family, if it could be avoided?

Ari Thór hadn't done anything wrong, not exactly. He had become a good father, warm and conscientious. It was clear that he would make every effort to ensure that his son would grow up in a happy environment.

It had clearly never occurred to him that Kristín had thoughts of leaving. It was, however, an option she had been considering at length in the last few weeks, weighing up the pros and cons with cool detachment.

The arrival of the doctor had brought her dilemma to the surface. Of course he was part of the problem, to an extent; maybe she wanted to find out if it was a relationship that could work. She felt that she was in with a chance with this man, and a good chance at that. Or maybe she was making more out of this than was really there?

She was determined not to make any move in that direction, not unless she had ended the relationship with Ari Thór first. If she was going to jump off this particular precipice, then there would be no parachute. Being unfaithful to Ari Thór was not something she could contemplate. It simply wasn't in her nature to cheat; unlike him.

He had been unfaithful to her with that local tart, Ugla. Just a kiss, he had said, but that was more than enough. She could see the guilt in his eyes when he begged her forgiveness. She knew him too well.

She hardly dared to imagine Ari Thór's reaction if she left him and immediately started a relationship with another man. Would he be able to control his rage? In all honesty, she wasn't sure that he could. There was some dark thread running through his character that was best avoided: he was quick to anger and capable of almost pathological jealousy. With time, could she help him overcome this basic fault in his character?

It wasn't that she felt unsafe around him and the thought that he might do her harm was out of the question. If she was in any danger, then he was there to protect her and would undoubtedly go to any extreme necessary.

But there were those *secrets* of his. After all these years, he had never told her the truth about his father's disappearance, and he had to know more about that than he had ever admitted. He clearly didn't trust her completely. She knew that this preyed on his mind, sometimes he would call out to his father in his sleep, in a voice so heart-achingly desperate…

Kristín was still some way from making up her mind and the past weeks had been difficult ones, keeping her awake at night as she tried to put her thoughts and feelings in some kind of order, weighing up the advantages and disadvantages in credit and debit columns, but unable to reach a conclusion.

The assault on Herjólfur had opened her eyes to just how short life could be, and how crucial it was to take the right decisions. If she was going to leave Ari Thór, then she would have to make her move, and soon.

Ari Thór and Tómas were still at the police station, and it was approaching dinnertime. The phone had rung without respite all day, and Tómas handled most of the media calls in his usual clipped, formal manner.

Tómas switched on the police station's small television set. The evening news bulletin was devoted almost entirely to the shooting in Siglufjördur.

'You'd best get yourself off home soon,' Tómas said. 'I'll keep watch for a while and we'll go to the scene in the morning. Our forensic colleagues tell me that they don't have all that much left to do. Have you been inside that house before?'

Ari Thór shook his head and reached for a slice of pizza. Tómas had gone down to the town hall square to his favourite pizza place and brought back a couple of hot ones.

'You can't beat a Siglufjördur pizza,' he said, tomato sauce streaked across his chin.

Ari Thór felt a twinge of conscience at not having been home to see Kristín since the morning. It wasn't far, but he hoped she would understand.

'I'll take a couple of slices home for Kristín if there's any left over.'

'Of course. Help yourself. How's the little one?'

'Fine,' he said before realising that Tómas had been fishing for a more extensive answer. 'He's like a tank, crawling everywhere, and he's doing his best to stand up. He's not talking, just burbles and laughs. I'm trying to explain to him that Christmas is coming, and I've bought far too many presents for him.'

Tómas broke into a smile. 'I ought to meet the lad while I'm here.'

'Definitely.'

'My wife has knitted him a jumper, and hopefully it will fit. We were going to send it before Christmas. A shame that I was in such a hurry to get here I didn't get a chance to bring it with me.'

'She knitted him a jumper? That's too much, Tómas. Thank you.'

'Don't mention it. Not that I had much to do with it, never having knitted a thing,' he said with a smile. 'We need to arrange to have you for dinner when there's an opportunity. When are you likely to be in the south next?'

'We don't have any plans, but Kristín's parents are moving home from Norway next summer and I expect the three of us will be down to see them often enough.'

'And how have you and Herjólfur been managing, considering there are only two of you?'

'It's working out, but only just, we get some assistance from the station along the coast in Ólafsfjördur,' Ari Thór replied.

He had missed his talks with Tómas, realising that he probably had only two good friends now, Kristín and Tómas. After moving to Siglufjördur he had more or less lost contact with his old friends in Reykjavík, and he hadn't really made any in Siglufjördur, except for Tómas. Of course there was Ugla, who still lived in the town, but they hadn't spoken for years. She had shown him the door when she had found out he already had a girlfriend, and now he wouldn't dare even look at her, knowing how Kristín would react.

Tómas glanced at a desk on which there was nothing but a computer and a keyboard.

'Nobody's taken Hlynur's place yet, I see,' he said heavily.

'No. Not yet.'

Hlynur, along with with Ari Thór and Tómas, had been Siglufjördur's police force, until he had taken his own life in the middle of a difficult murder investigation. Ari Thór knew that Tómas had never recovered fully from the shock, and still blamed himself to some extent for what had happened. Ari Thór also felt he deserved some of the blame for not having made an effort to connect with his colleague when there was obviously something troubling him, but then again Ari Thór had been the new boy in town and most of his focus had been on settling in.

Tómas's mobile phone rang a moment later and Ari Thór could see from his expression that something had happened.

It was a short conversation and as soon as it was over, Tómas hurried over to the computer.

'Come here, will you, Ari Thór?' He spoke gruffly, worry etched on his brow.

Ari Thór was in no state to be on duty. The multitude of concerns that were spinning in his mind, his illness, his confusion about the case, meant that any energy he had left was fast running out and fatigue was gaining the upper hand. There was little he could do and he had to keep going.

'What is it?' he sighed, wiping his brow and making his way over to his old friend.

'Look at this,' Tómas said, his finger pointing at the computer screen. 'We've been sent the list of numbers Herjólfur called before he was assaulted, as well as the numbers from which he was called. Sit down and look them up. You're quicker than I am.'

Tómas stood up and let Ari Thór sit at the computer. 'Start with this one. That's the last number to call Herjólfur's phone.'

Ari Thór searched without success. 'It's an unregistered number.'

'In that case we'll ask for more information,' Tómas said. 'Other numbers called, that sort of thing.'

'I'll send a request,' Ari Thór said wearily. The rain pounded at the window, hammering a staccato beat that matched his growing headache. The station was hot and a long night beckoned. Ari Thór knew Kristín would not be pleased. Her recent detachment was unsettling, but he hadn't had the courage to investigate its cause.

He continued to search through the most recent calls. Most were innocuous, a few calls to Herjólfur's wife, some to Ari Thór's own number, and one call to a restaurant in Reykjavík.

'He was going to take his wife off to Reykjavík,' Ari Thór

explained. 'He mentioned it because he wanted to be sure I'd be well enough to be back on duty. The trip was supposed to be a surprise for her. She probably doesn't know about it, Helena. Maybe I should have told her…' Ari Thór said more to himself than to Tómas. 'But this one is worth looking into.'

'What's that?'

Tómas came over to see for himself.

'Gunnar Gunnarsson, the mayor.'

'He called Herjólfur?' Tómas asked, squinting at the screen.

'No. Herjólfur called him, two days ago.'

'There has to be a reasonable explanation,' Tómas said, cautious as usual.

'Late in the evening,' Ari Thór said.

'What?'

'He called him at just about ten in the evening. That's a strange time to call a town official.'

Tómas nodded. 'I agree. Maybe we should go and knock on his door. Best to do it now rather than waiting until tomorrow, wouldn't you say?'

Ari Thór shrugged. He still felt a need to prove himself to Tómas.

'Suits me,' he said, against his own better judgement. He was so very, very tired. Most of all he wanted to go home, climb into bed, and deal with everything later; the case, Tómas's demands, Kristín's recent behaviour.

'Email about that unregistered number first,' Tómas decided. 'Then we'll go for a drive before I let you go home and get some sleep. You look like you could certainly do with it.'

Ari Thór was uncomfortably warm, but refreshing volleys of raindrops against the misted glass of the station windows offered some potential respite. This was his job, and he had to do it, but his instincts told him that this was not going to be a straightforward visit, and that something dark was simmering at the heart of Siglufjördur. Someone had tried to murder a police officer in cold blood. They were in uncharted territory, nothing like this had ever

happened. There was no way of knowing whether or when the assailant would strike again and Ari Thór was frightened.

According to the nurse, Dr Helgi won't be here until tomorrow. She'll find out if he can see me then.

It's not easy to work out her age, and I can't bring myself to ask her. Maybe around forty. She has a slightly pudgy face; too much red wine and too many steaks over the years. Her eyes are tired and she never smiles. I can't get on with people who don't smile.

It may well be that she's not even forty, and if that's the case then she hasn't looked after herself. She's not my type, that's for certain.

There's something about her that I don't like, a coldness behind her eyes.

I can't write much about my roommate because he never says a thing and doesn't do much other than sleep. The only good thing about having him in front of me all day is that he's a sort of encouragement to shake off the lethargy. Yes, I'll go to tomorrow's morning meeting. Maybe I'll find out the truth.

The mayor lived in a detached house on a new estate on the land-ward side of the fjord.

It was a while before anyone came to the door and when he did, the mayor was dressed in a white dressing gown and matching slip-pers. There was a look of astonishment on his face when he saw the two police officers, but he hastily rearranged his features into an expectant, friendly expression.

'Gunnar?' Tómas asked, with his usual courtesy.

'That's me,' he said, with a standard-issue politician's smile on his lips.

'My name's Tómas and I was the inspector in charge of the local force here for many years. That was before your time, of course.' His voice was laden with authority. 'I expect you're already familiar with Ari Thór?'

'Of course. Come in, boys. Apologies that I'm not dressed for the occasion, but I wasn't expecting guests. This is how it is when you live alone.'

They followed him into the living room. The television was on and the remnants of what looked to be a forlorn microwave meal were on the table.

'I'd offer you something, but I have to admit that the cupboard is pretty bare. This is a sort of bachelor existence,' he said, his apology sounding artificial. 'My wife's working abroad. She's a doctor.'

He offered them the sofa, without taking a seat himself.

'What's the news?' He asked. 'How is Herjólfur? He's still … with us?'

'He is,' Tómas replied, and paused.

'Thank God for that. It's a terrible thing to happen. It's hard to understand it. The atmosphere at the Town Hall today was very subdued, to say the least, and most people left early. Damn it…' he swore, his voice rising. 'I can't believe that a police officer has been gunned down here in Siglufjördur.'

Ari Thór looked at Tómas, hoping that he would interrupt before Gunnar broke into a political rant about the safety of police officers on duty. Tómas didn't let him down, and went straight to the point.

'Why did Herjólfur call you two days ago?'

'We're both on the traffic safety committee,' Gunnar answered quickly, almost before Tómas had finished his question, like a well-prepared contestant in a quiz. 'There were a few things he wanted to discuss.'

'Such as?' Tómas asked, adopting the same carefree tone.

'Mainly the roundabout and a few other matters that we need to discuss at the next meeting,' Gunnar replied smoothly, without apparently needing to think. 'I don't recall precisely what was said, as I have a lot on my plate. It's a busy job.'

A roundabout? Ari Thór wondered if the man couldn't have come up with a more convincing lie.

'What roundabout?' Tómas asked. 'There's a roundabout in Siglufjördur now? That's some impressive progress in the short time since I moved south.'

Ari Thór kept himself deliberately to one side. He preferred to maintain a decent relationship with the mayor, and this conversation looked like it was going to end badly.

'Well, not exactly. It's more about building roundabouts, to improve road safety. You understand?'

Tómas's expression demonstrated that he saw no point in building a roundabout in such a small town.

'It reduces speeding,' the mayor added haughtily, back in election mode, as he did his utmost to convince his audience.

'Speeding was never a problem when I was inspector here,' Tómas muttered, a little too loudly.

'No, maybe not. But now the town is opening up, with more through traffic, maybe a higher crime rate…'

'Why was this so important?' Tómas asked, his tone sharper than before.

'What do you mean?'

'Discussing roundabouts. It was after ten at night when Herjólfur called you.'

This time Gunnar hesitated.

'I couldn't say why the man decided to call me so late. I recall that I found it intrusive at the time. As you can see, I'm not much of a one for staying up late.' He smiled and looked down at the dressing gown. 'I didn't say anything to him about it, of course. I was just my usual courteous self. We had built up a good working relationship.'

'Did you discuss any other matters?'

'I honestly don't remember.'

'Was that the last time you and he spoke?'

'Yes, yes, it was. But I couldn't have known at the time what was about to happen, so it wasn't an especially memorable conversation. And I hope it doesn't turn out to have been our last conversation.'

A pretty weak hope, Ari Thór thought to himself, recalling the harrowing scene upon which he had arrived only that morning. It seemed days ago now, the horror of it still thrumming away at the corners of his mind, muted only by his determined effort to keep it there.

'Did he say anything about the house?' Tómas asked.

'The house?'

'The house where the shooting took place.'

Tómas's voice was measured. Gunnar appeared increasingly agitated.

'Well, why would he have done that?' Gunnar asked. Tómas's silence was deafening. 'Of course he didn't mention that house,' Gunnar snapped at last.

Tómas rose quickly to his feet and Ari Thór followed his lead.

'Thank you for the information and apologies for the intrusion.'

'What? Yes, of course. A shame I can't be of more help.'

'Maybe later.'

'Well, precisely. Yes.'

'Don't hesitate to get in touch, Gunnar, if there's anything that occurs to you.'

They left the mayor in his dressing gown, standing in his living room.

'Now I'm taking you home,' Tómas said when they were in the car.

'That would be kind,' Ari Thór said, unable to keep the fatigue out of his voice.

'What did you make of your mayor's performance?' Tómas asked, glancing over at his dishevelled colleague.

Ari Thór paused. 'I've never seen him lie so obviously,' he said quietly. 'There's something he's not telling us, and I have a feeling it has more than a little to do with Herjólfur's shooting.'

10

Gunnar sat still for a while after the police officers had gone. He had expected questions about that phone call, but not right away and not with such vigour.

He had kept himself dry for twelve years but there were still occasions when he felt that a drop would help; just enough to settle his nerves. This wasn't the first time he had been tempted, nor was it the worst situation he'd faced over those twelve years, and he knew he would get over it.

Loneliness had become more of a burden that he liked to admit. The days at work weren't a problem, but in the evenings when he came home, the cold, empty house, far too big for him, was all there was to receive him. The job was demanding and he relished the involvement in municipal politics, working out the cliques and establishing how people would form alliances on particular issues. It was certainly an advantage for the municipality to have an outsider in his position, someone with no allegiances. In the same way it was a clever move to bring in an outsider to manage the investigation. He was sure that Ari Thór on his own would never have dared to push his way into the mayor's residence to make veiled accusations so late in the evening.

He stood up and drew the curtains, an unconscious reaction to the police's invasion of his home. He also managed to shut out the darkness outside, but there was no hiding from the sound of the rain. What a miserable day this had been, in every respect. The low pressure that was bringing them all this October rain also had a negative effect on Gunnar's mood that he felt very deeply.

He switched on the espresso machine. Normally he avoided coffee in the evenings, but he suspected he wouldn't sleep much anyway.

He wanted to call his wife, not to tell her about the visit from the police, but more to make some kind of contact. It wasn't too late for a call to Norway, but the relationship had become so strained that phone calls for no special reason had long ago been consigned to the past. She would be surprised to hear from him and would want a reason for the call, and then there would be silence on the line between Siglufjördur and Oslo.

Instead he called Elín. He wanted to go and see her, but couldn't bring himself to do it. An evening visit could result in all kinds of awkward misunderstandings. There was no point in boosting the inevitable gossip that was undoubtedly already being whispered about the mayor and his deputy.

She answered quickly, as she did everything. Sharp-witted and astute, Elín responded rapidly to anything he asked her to do at work.

'I just had a visit from the police,' he blurted out, not bothering with any courtesies.

'A visit? At your place?' Elín asked.

'Yes.'

'And … what did they want to know?' she asked, her voice guarded.

'Why Herjólfur called me the day before yesterday,' he replied, trying to hide his worries.

There was silence on the line.

'And what did you tell them?' Elín finally asked.

'What we decided, of course.'

'And they believed you?'

'Well, I think so. Yes, I'm sure they did.'

The silence deepened. He knew what was at stake, and how unlikely it was that this was the last they would hear of it.

This is the first day that nobody has been sitting outside my room.

Of course they were checking that I didn't do myself any harm. Fortunately they let me have a little elbow room. The door was kept ajar and I was able to go to the toilet and the shower by myself.

I wouldn't have tried anything, even with nobody watching. At the moment I want to continue to live, in spite of being frightened, as always.

I seem to be past the worst, judging by the fact that I'm not being watched every moment of the day, like a small child.

This morning's meeting wasn't too bad. The staff and the inmates all talked as equals, on the surface, naturally. There wasn't a doctor to be seen, any more than any other day. Doctors seem to be a rare sight on the ward. There were nurses, medical staff and some auxiliary staff there. I'm not quite sure who does what. Nobody wears a uniform but you can normally tell the staff by the keys they have in their hands all the time.

I didn't say anything at the meeting, just listened. The discussion was mostly about the programme for the day. It's the height of summer and most of them wanted to be out in the gardens. I have to stay indoors for a few more days, or so I'm told. All the same, I'd have liked to have gone outside in the warm weather. It's hot, stuffy – airless in here. There's a balcony, a smart little one, at the end of the corridor. I'd love to be able to go out there, breathe the fresh air and enjoy the sunshine for a little while, but the doors are kept locked. That balcony is like a mirage in the desert.

The meeting became almost amusing this morning, when the other inmates started complaining about each other. One asked to be moved to another room as the man he was sharing with is bad-tempered and borderline violent. The other guy answered right back, so forcefully that it confirmed the first one's point. They carried on for a while without reaching any conclusion. The staff didn't seem concerned about chasing the inmates' minor complaints, but an argument like that must serve *some purpose. It clears the air, gives people an opportunity to air pent-up grievances without coming to blows. The blows come later.*

11

Ari Thór slept badly that night. He woke up more than once, finding it hard to fall asleep again with the heavy rain beating on the roof of the old house. His home was usually warm and cosy, a safe haven, but now it just felt cold and menacing.

The flu was to blame as much as the assault on Herjólfur. The incident had been a shock, but the thought of how narrowly he had avoided being the target ... If he hadn't been ill...

It wasn't just his concern about Herjólfur that kept him awake. If he was honest with himself, he had not been able to create any real relationship with his new superior. Of course he hoped that the inspector would make a full recovery, and at the very least survive. It was unthinkable that any police officer should lose his life under such circumstances, and it didn't matter who the victim was. And now that he had met Herjólfur's wife and son, Ari Thór felt a bewildering set of new sympathies for his colleague's family.

He and Tómas had sat in stifling silence on the short drive home, the rain outside a premonition of the arrival of winter. Ever since that first winter in Siglufjördur, Ari Thór always felt slightly claustrophobic when the snow started falling heavily, even though the new tunnel meant that it was almost impossible to be snowbound in the town any longer. Kristín was already asleep by the time he returned home, and he didn't try to wake her.

The next morning they both woke around six, as usual, when Stefnir began to make his presence felt by crying. At first the sounds he made were soft, and there was still a chance that he might fall back asleep if they left him alone, but eventually he was fully awake and demanding attention. They were both due at work, so Stefnir would be cared for by a childminder who lived nearby, an amiable older lady approved by Kristín. It was never easy to leave the boy with a stranger, but there was no choice in the matter.

Kristín was unusually reserved that morning, although it was something Ari Thór had become used to over the last few weeks. Exhaustion clouding his usual, uneasy acceptance, he looked out at the relentless downpour, frost tickling the edges of the windows, a smog of condensation veiling their centres and, somehow, he felt, his own relationship.

'Is everything all right, Kristín?'

'Of course, yes,' she replied, without meeting his eyes.

He waited a moment for a plausible explanation, glanced at her and looked away. He stirred the cereal in his bowl and pushed this exchange to the back of his mind, as he'd become accustomed to doing.

⊕

Tómas collected Ari Thór and they drove out to the old house by the tunnel.

'I've been in touch with the technical division,' Tómas said as he parked close to where Herjólfur's car had been found. ' They have nothing yet to indicate who might be behind the attack.'

'That figures,' said Ari Thór. 'I didn't expect anything so soon.' He was feeling brighter now; the flu was subsiding, although the fatigue had still not retreated.

'It's a long time since I've been up here to this old place,' Tómas said thoughtfully as they approached the derelict building, which looked almost like a real-life haunted house to Ari Thór. It must have been an imposing building in the past, but a complete lack of maintenance left it dilapidated and almost menacing. The house seemed to have an aura of death about it, regardless of the shooting, thought Ari Thór. The local kids probably avoided it, but it was the perfect place for shady drug deals. Its location on the edge of the cliff only added to the sense of danger that emanated from its crumbling walls.

'I'm not even sure if I dare work out how many years ago it was. I had to deal with the poor old guy who moved himself in here after the place had been abandoned,' Tómas continued.

'When was that?'

'Around 1980, if I remember correctly. The surviving twin stayed on but I gather he only used part of the house, and then let it fall into disrepair. He was a relatively young man when he died, and after that nobody bothered fixing the place up. It would hardly have been worth it. Property prices in Siglufjördur haven't been great for decades – you know this, Ari Thór – ever since the herring disappeared. Things are only starting to pick up, and it has never been the most popular part of the town, too far from the centre.'

It crossed Ari Thór's mind that although it would need a lot of work, if the place were to be fixed up properly, it could possibly be an attractive place to rent out to tourists. The setting was magnificent, on the outer end of the fjord, and with a wonderful view when the weather was fine enough to provide visibility.

They went through the front door into a chilly hallway. Ari Thór was slightly reluctant to go inside, but he wouldn't allow himself to show any weakness. It was just a house, after all, even though it was now the setting of two horrible events, the mysterious death of the twin and the attempted killing of Herjólfur. Ari Thór flicked the light switch, but there appeared to be no power in the building. Then again he hadn't expected any such luxury.

'Careful, Ari Thór,' Tómas said, taking a torch from his pocket. 'The living room's here to the left. Most of the windows were broken long ago. The local kids had a fine time throwing stones through them after the owner died. This place is in the state it is because of human activity as well as nature.'

Tómas shone his torch around the living room. Ari Thór could see a rickety table, stained and lacking a coat of varnish, and some worn-out chairs.

'Didn't anyone take the furniture after the owner died?'

'It doesn't look like it. I couldn't say what went on, but I suspect that anything of any value must have been taken.'

'The gunman must have stood here,' Ari Thór said. 'Herjólfur was on the ground just outside.'

'Exactly. The technical division came to the same conclusion. There was no evidence of a warning shot or anything like that. Shall we take a look upstairs?'

Ari Thór followed Tómas up the decrepit staircase that creaked with every footstep, reminding him of ice about to crack underfoot on a frozen pond. He stepped gingerly, intent on avoiding a tumble on the stairs. He held tight to the handrail, quickly letting go of it when he felt it coming adrift from the wall.

'This is where he lived, the brother who survived. His name was Börkur. They were the twins, Börkur and Baldur,' Tómas said, indicating a small room next to the landing.

The beam of the torch illuminated a bed and a bedside table next to it.

'This is where the drunk was living the last time I came here,' Tómas continued. 'He didn't seem to be frightened to be bedding down here.'

'Frightened?'

'Yes, this is where Baldur died, or rather, fell off the balcony,' Tómas said, shining the beam of torchlight to flicker over the balcony doors.

'Can we get out onto the balcony?' Ari Thór asked.

'No idea. Give it a try.'

The door's hinges complained, but gave way all the same. Ari Thór squeezed himself out onto the tiny balcony. He gazed out into the morning and his thoughts inexplicably returned to Kristín. *Had he done something wrong? Why was she behaving so strangely?*

'How old is this place?' he called in to Tómas.

'I'm not sure. Built around 1930, I'd guess, and solidly. Their father was a fisherman who did well for himself, but after he drowned, the boys were brought up by their mother. She never remarried.'

'You can tell from the balcony.'

'What?' Tómas appeared in the doorway.

'The age of the house. Today nobody would dream of building a balcony with a railing that low. It's an accident waiting to happen.'

'That's just where he fell off.'

Ari Thór had no desire to go the same way and quickly shut the doors behind him as he came back inside.

'Are they all dead?'

'All?'

'Baldur, Börkur and their friend. Didn't you say there were three of them here when Baldur died?'

Ari Thór tried to imagine what kind of party might have taken place almost half a century ago but found it difficult to visualise.

'Yes, you're right. They're all gone now, the brothers and their friend,' Tómas said absently. 'But their friend's sister, Jódís, is still with us. She's very much alive, at seventy-four.'

Ari Thór had a strange feeling about this sinister house, and an inexplicable urge to flee. But he was also sure that there was a mystery here to be solved. Whether or not it had a direct bearing on last night's shooting, he couldn't tell. Yet…

12

Herjólfur's wife Helena and their son were due to travel south with a police officer. Herjólfur's condition remained critical, and he was being kept in an induced coma in intensive care.

'We'll have a word with her before she goes,' Tómas had suggested, and here they were. They stood at the door for a while. Tómas had already rung the bell twice and knocked hard before a muffled 'come in' could be heard from inside.

They entered cautiously. This was the second time in two days that Ari Thór had been inside his superior officer's house and he led the way to the living room, reflecting again that the house belonged to a man about whom he knew virtually nothing at all. Helena was still seated on the pristine white sofa and, in the background, Ari Thór could hear a Brahms lullaby – a piece that he knew well.

Helena seemed to know instinctively what he was thinking, and she looked up through a mask of exhaustion.

'It was Herjólfur's favourite,' she said, as if reciting a meaningless fact, her words bereft of any emotion. 'I'll have it played at the funeral.'

Her words took Ari Thór by surprise. She appeared to have given up all hope.

'Do you mind if we sit down?' Tómas asked politely.

'Of course not. Are you driving us south?'

'No, not me,' Tómas said in a slow voice. 'Another officer will drive you. He'll be here in half an hour. We just wanted a word with you before you leave.'

She attempted another smile. 'Of course. I know you,' she said, pointing at Ari Thór. 'But who are you?' she asked, her question directed at Tómas.

'My name's Tómas. I was the inspector in charge here before your husband took over.'

'Ah, Tómas. Right. Herjólfur mentioned your name. Have you come back to take over again?'

'Far from it. I'm simply here to manage the investigation.'

The music stopped. There was a short pause and the same piece of music began to play again.

'It's beautiful,' Helena said. 'He appreciated good music and literature.' She continued to use the past tense to refer to her husband.

'I understand that Herjólfur was investigating a case linked to the house, the place where he was … assaulted,' Ari Thór said cautiously. 'Do you know anything about that?'

'No, I can't say that I do. We didn't talk much about that kind of thing, Herjólfur and I. He didn't talk about his work.'

'Do you recall anything that could give us any clue about his attack?' Tómas probed.

'Clue…' she said slowly, as if turning the word over in her mind. 'I haven't thought about it. There's no going back, anyway. Wasn't it just some terrible coincidence?' She looked blankly at Ari Thór. 'It could just as easily have been you,' she added.

Ari Thór shivered.

'I'm sorry, but can I ask something?' she said deferentially. 'Will I get any compensation? I mean enough to support the family? How does this work in the police? I just don't know that I could go out and work now…' She sighed. 'I stopped working not long after we met and I had a fall from a horse and broke my leg badly. Herjólfur has supported us all since then. I just don't know…'

'Don't worry. We look after our own,' Tómas said encouragingly, and it was as if a burden had been lifted from Helena's shoulders. 'And we can also still hope it will turn out for the best,' he added, but with little conviction in his words.

'Is he in a hurry, the gentleman who is taking us to Reykjavík?

It's just that my son is coming as well and he went out to the shop.'

'That won't be a problem,' Tómas replied.

She forced a smile. 'Well, that's good to know. He might be back already. He's living in the flat in the basement so he can come and go when it suits him. We don't see much of him. He's got a girlfriend now, and he'll have flown the nest before we know it,' she added sorrowfully, with the same wan smile.

'Your husband had been on leave for some time before you moved here. Is that right?'

For the first time, Helena hesitated for a second.

'I've been ill,' she said slowly, as if unwilling to discuss the matter. 'I was suffering from depression. Herjólfur took time off to look after me.'

'I'm sorry to hear that,' Tómas said, sounding awkward. 'I hope you've made a full recovery.' He stood up.

She smiled at him again, a somewhat meaningless expression. Ari Thór wondered whether she had actually made a full recovery from her depression, or whether the shock had perhaps caused her to relapse. She shifted uncomfortably on the white sofa, moving one leg awkwardly and grimacing as she tried to make herself comfortable.

'Thank you for coming. Since yesterday everything has been very unreal. Not many people have called and nobody has been to see us. People don't want to intrude. Not that we know many people here. It was good to see you. I'm sorry if I haven't been much help.'

'Don't worry. We'll look after things. We have a big team working on this, our best people, and you can be sure that we'll get to the bottom of it,' Tómas said firmly, leaving no doubt that he was completely serious.

'I should have offered you some coffee…' Helena apologised. 'I'm sorry, that was thoughtless of me.'

'Don't even think of it,' Tómas said. 'I just hope the news is better when you get down south.'

Ari Thór had no such optimism. He was certain that it was only a matter of time before this would turn into a murder investigation, and he felt that he somehow owed it to Herjólfur's family to put all his efforts into trying to find the killer.

To tell the truth, today has been something of a difficult day. It's not easy being shut up in here in this heat. It certainly wasn't my intention to spend the summer like this, now that my year off is starting. This is the time I had planned to use to travel and to decide on a direction in life. I can see easily enough what the conclusion is likely to be and I don't have a lot of choice in the matter. But there's no harm in having dreams.

Speaking of dreams, last night I dreamt that I was learning to play the piano. I haven't played since I was a child. I'm not sure if I heard the tune in my dream or not; probably not, but of course I know it well. When I woke up, the tune was echoing in my head and it appears to have taken root there. It's a pleasant sensation, having a melody on your mind all day long. It's a piece of music that has long been a favourite of mine, but everything's best in moderation.

Nobody has come to visit me yet. I know that Mum couldn't handle it, so I couldn't make any demands on her. She's not always been strong. Dad made it crystal clear when I was admitted that he wouldn't be visiting for a while. He said I'd need time to get over it. Then he glared at the doctor and asked if that was sensible. The doctor just shrugged carelessly and glanced at the clock as if he had run out of time for me.

Hanna won't be paying me a visit, that's for sure. I don't imagine she'll want to see me again. I guess she'll be pleased when she hears I've been locked up in a psychiatric ward. Good lord … locked up in a psychiatric ward. It doesn't look good when it's written down, but that's the way it is.

But I can take comfort in knowing that I don't belong here…

On the other hand, don't all the inmates think that?

Dinner was fairly tasteless, which isn't all that bad considering what it looked like. At some point this unappetising stew was fish, although I couldn't tell what sort of fish it had been, or how long ago.

Maybe I ought to try and read during the day. There are a few books available, but I've made a point of not making myself too comfortable here. This isn't going to be a long stay. I doubt there'll be much there that's to my taste anyhow. I have good taste, a refined taste that's undoubtedly unusual for someone of my age. Thórbergur Thórdarson, Halldór Laxness, Ernest Hemingway, those are my guys.

I wanted to study literature at university but I don't have a choice in the matter. There's a path already carved out for me and I fear what the future will bring. I have to break out of myself, if that's the right expression. I don't even know if I can, and have even less idea whether or not this is the right place to do it.

I'm tired now. I expect to meet Dr Helgi tomorrow to talk about how bad I feel. Maybe things will get better. It's good to be optimistic.

The book can go to its usual hiding place under the mattress. No one sees it. It holds my secrets.

13

Elín didn't bother to knock any more. She opened the door carefully and peered around it.

Gunnar noticed her straightaway. He didn't let this over-familiarity irritate him, although he would have preferred her to maintain a more professional distance during working hours.

'How are things, Elín? Take a seat,' he said amiably.

She shut the door behind her.

'I just wanted to see how you are,' she said warmly, her eyes searching his face as she sat opposite him. He was behind his desk, the mayor's desk. It was a magnificent piece of furniture, totally out of keeping with every other item in the office, which might have been ordered from a clearance sale catalogue in the mid-nineties, and never replaced.

'Not so bad. Keeping busy.' He averted his eyes.

In fact, the police visit had preyed on his mind to the exclusion of almost everything else all day. But he wasn't going to admit it.

He leaned back in his chair and lifted his feet to rest them on the desk, emphasising the fact that he wasn't concerned, and to remind himself that he was still a young rebel at heart, even though he now wore a suit.

'Come on, you're not fooling me,' she said softly.

'I'm not trying to fool anyone.' He took a deep breath. 'Have they spoken to you?' he asked eventually.

'No, of course not. And you know well enough that I wouldn't tell them anything.'

'I'm sorry. It's just so awkward. This Tómas character is so pushy, although he avoided being outright rude. It's as if he really thinks I had something to do with ... the incident.' He dropped his feet to the floor and stood up. 'Goddammit, this is not something I'm prepared to put up with,' he said, bringing his open palm down on the desk with a louder bang than he had intended.

Elín was on her feet in an instant and went over to him, placing a hand on his shoulder and pushing him back into the chair.

'Relax. It'll be fine.'

'This is my big chance, you understand?' he said, hysteria teetering on the edge of his voice, and for a moment he felt as if he were speaking to his wife. 'This is my stepping stone. I'd never have had a chance of a job like this without the right connections, and a bit of luck. And I'm not going to screw this up.'

She stood behind him and massaged his shoulders.

'Don't let it upset you. The police are in a panic. A police inspector murdered, or as good as, and a killer on the loose.'

Her hands shifted to stroke his neck lightly and Gunnar wasn't sure how to react. It felt good – too good, but he didn't see any reason to complain, not right away, at least. He wasn't doing anything wrong, just sitting there. He couldn't be accused of being unprofessional.

She continued to talk, and her fingers didn't stop.

'We're due to be at a harbour board meeting later today, but I'll postpone it so you can take some time off. I have to go up to the valley anyway to see people about some planning changes for the ski area, and that might take all day.'

Then what Gunnar had feared and also hoped for happened. She kissed him gently on the neck. He waited for a moment, letting the joy of it infuse him before he turned round.

'Listen, we shouldn't go too far,' he said awkwardly, his thoughts suddenly shifting to his wife in Norway.

'Yes, I'm sorry.' Elín let her hands fall to her sides. 'I'm sorry,' she repeated. She looked anything but.

14

When Kristín was finally able to take a break, she saw that she had missed five calls from her mother.

Three pre-lunch calls were nothing unusual, a testament to her mother's occasional lack of patience when there was something she badly needed to talk about. But five missed calls meant that Kristín had no choice but to call her back, even if it was unlikely that anything was wrong. Her mother loved being at the centre of a drama, which was a significant difference in their natures. Kristín was undoubtedly more like her father, pragmatic, thoughtful and quiet.

Five calls with no hint as to what they were about – that was her mother all over. A text or even a voicemail would never convey the full import of whatever was on her mother's mind. The spoken word was her preferred form of communication, and Kristín steeled herself for the inevitable over-excitement that was bound to follow.

'Kristín!' her mother replied, picking up her phone instantly. There was no ordinary 'hello', just a full-volume cry instead.

'Hi, Mum,' she said, weary already.

'So what's new, my dear?'

Kristín was exhausted. Although the boy would wake her occasionally, it was her worries about her relationship with Ari Thór that were preventing her from sleeping at night. She had to resolve that one way or another, but she wasn't going to share this with her mother.

'Everything's fine, Mum. Everything's just fine.'

'Of course it is. Is Stefnir there? Is that him I can hear?'

'No, Mum. That's the PA system at the hospital. He's with the childminder today.'

Kristín sighed. Yet another phone call about nothing at all.

'You're at work? Aren't you working too hard, sweetheart?' her mother demanded, the concern clear in her voice.

'I'm just starting back after maternity leave, but it's all right. We all have to work.'

'Of course. But you and Ari Thór are fine?'

'Yes, Mum. We're doing fine.'

'Ah,' her mother breathed, her voice full of pleasure. 'You are such a lovely couple, it's as if you were made for each other. He's just the right type for you, Kristín. You're going to have to let him take you down that aisle soon. You can't let such a good man go.' Her mother gave voice to her standard polite laughter. 'That child is so lucky to have such reliable parents and such a strong family, just like you did. It makes such a difference when a child's parents are happy together.'

It was as if her mother had pierced her heart.

'Well, Mum…' Kristín said, desperate to talk about something else. She looked at the clock, determined not to spend her entire break on the phone.

'Yes, darling. It's always good to hear your voice.'

'And you, Mum? Was there anything special? I saw you called a couple of times this morning.'

'That's right, I wanted to let you know that we're coming home early,' she declared, joy pervading every word of her announcement.

'You're moving back?'

'Yes, we've booked flights and we'll arrive in two weeks. I've already given notice at my office and your father got his employers to agree to let him work on preparing the Icelandic office *from* Iceland instead of working on it in Norway.'

Kristín's father had been a fishing industry consultant in Norway after losing his job in the wake of the financial crash, and was now working for an expanding Norwegian company. Not so long ago it had been Iceland's meteoric expansion abroad, but things had changed dramatically. Her mother was an architect and had easily found work in Norway.

'I thought you weren't coming until the summer?'

'We're just too keen to see you and to spend some time with our little prince, of course.' There was a moment's silence. 'Naturally, we've been following the news on the radio…'

Kristín knew that her parents followed every detail of Icelandic news from Norway. The first thing she had done the previous day, before the incident hit the papers, was to call her parents and reassure them that the injured police officer was not their son-in-law.

'This attack is getting so much coverage it's terrifying. This is so unbelievable, Kristín, someone shooting a police officer. In Iceland! They say it's the first time ever anyone has taken a shot at the police, and I think they're right. Never in my life could I have imagined this. I always thought Iceland was the safest place on earth … Anyway, it gave us something of a wake-up call … It feels wrong to be so far away when such awful things are happening. Ari Thór must be having a terrible time right now.'

'Yes, of course he is.'

'I just wanted you to know. We're so excited to be coming home.'

'We're excited to see you as well,' Kristín said. She certainly missed her parents but, nonetheless, she felt a knot of worry forming in her belly at the thought of their imminent return. *Things were not quite as rosy as her mother made out.*

Who the hell had the bright idea that this screamingly bright orange would go down well with the inmates on a psychiatric ward? The mattress is orange and so is the chair. The door is dark brown, creating a colour scheme from hell. I can't be happy in here and I have no desire to mix with the people on the other side of the door.

I'm in a dreadful mood today. I spoke to the nurse and asked her when I could have an appointment with Dr Helgi.

Not now, she said. Not this week. Short and cold. She doesn't like me. It was as if she was telling me about the weather rather than breaking the news that I wouldn't be able to see my doctor this week. How am I supposed to make any progress? I must see him.

Why not? I asked. I must have sounded angrier than usual, and I was furious.

I saw her take a step back. Was she frightened of me? Maybe I was too brusque?

He doesn't want to see you right away, she replied. You need more time and he's very busy, but I've spoken to him on your behalf. And then she left me, none the wiser but a lot more unsettled.

15

Ari Thór was alone on duty after a long discussion with Tómas in front of the whiteboard.

Tómas had adopted some new habits since he'd left. He had become more formal and better organised, using the whiteboard at the police station to track the different threads of the investigation. Until now, the whiteboard had remained largely pristine.

No new information had been forthcoming and while there was little need for the meeting, Ari Thór had not protested. The only notable development was the fact that the owner of the mobile phone that had been used to call Herjólfur shortly before the attack could not be traced. The number was unregistered and the SIM card appeared to have been removed from the phone so it couldn't be tracked. The call had gone through a mast in Siglufjördur, but there was no possibility of pinpointing the caller's location with any real accuracy. This was the only call made, before or since, from that particular number.

'And I've requested the records of calls to and from your mayor,' Tómas added. 'It shouldn't take long.'

'Do you really think he…?' Ari Thór started to ask, before Tómas interrupted him.

'In the attempted murder of a police officer we don't rule anything out,' he said firmly.

After that, Tómas made himself scarce, saying he was going to call on Addi Gunna again.

'Best for you to stay here and keep things ticking over,' he said, a clear but discreet indication that he was more confident about getting something out of Addi if he went alone.

Left on his own in the station, Ari Thór's thoughts returned to Kristín. She'd called with the unexpected news that her parents were moving home to Iceland earlier than planned. He was genuinely pleased by this turn of events; not only did he like them, but he also enjoyed being part of a family. Their relationship was like nothing he had ever experienced in his upbringing. They might also be able to help out a bit, looking after Stefnir from time to time. Maybe he and Kristín would get a chance to go out for a meal or a film? Maybe the constant pressure was the reason for her odd behaviour? Ari Thór sighed and rubbed his temples with his thumbs. There was something wrong, and he didn't know if he had the strength to face up to it.

Ari Thór was startled by a knock on the police station window. He glanced out and saw a face he recognised, a history teacher from the local college. Ari Thór didn't know the man to speak to, but was getting to know many of the townspeople by sight. Anything else would have been virtually impossible in such a small community as Siglufjördur.

The teacher pointed, indicating the door, as if asking if he might come in, and Ari Thór nodded, standing up to greet his visitor.

'Good morning,' he said racking his brains for the man's name once the newcomer was inside the police station.

'Yes, hello,' he said, putting out a hand and introducing himself as he did so. 'Ingólfur.'

'Yes, I know,' Ari Thór said, trying to sound friendly. 'You teach at the college, don't you?'

'That's right, yes,' he said, and hesitated, as if he would prefer to be anywhere but standing in front of a local police officer. 'I teach history.'

Ari Thór waited for him to come to the point, while Ingólfur seemed to be looking for the right words.

'Well, I reckon…' he mumbled at last, as Ari Thór waited with growing impatience. 'I think Herjólfur might have been shot with my gun.'

16

Ingólfur buried his face in his hands, despair evident in his hunched shoulders. An unusually tall man, he was powerfully built, and well padded around the waist, someone who had once been fit, but let himself go.

After a short but painful silence, Ari Thór spoke.

'Sit down, won't you?'

Ingólfur looked up. 'What? Yes,' he murmured.

At first glance, he did not appear to be a man who might be able to keep the attention of young and unruly students, but it could be that being in the police station was unnerving him.

Ari Thór had planned to show him into the little meeting room that was sometimes referred to as the interview room, but Ingólfur had already taken him at his word and sat in the nearest chair, at Hlynur's old desk. There was something about the man that reminded him of Hlynur during the days and weeks before he took his own life. There had been a silence about him, and a worrying combination of hesitation, fear and distance.

'Well,' Ingólfur began, but the remaining words seemed to fade away.

Ari Thór waited patiently, recognising that it had been difficult for the man to find the courage to come down to the police station.

Ingólfur sighed deeply. 'Look, I'm sorry this is taking a while ... Someone borrowed my gun, or I think so, anyway. And it looks to me like it has been used...' He spoke swiftly, hardly pausing for breath.

'What makes you think someone has used your gun?' Ari Thór

asked gently. He had grabbed a recorder from his desk, setting it to record the interview.

'I noticed it yesterday, you understand? The gun was gone.'

'Yesterday, you say?' Ari Thór said in his usual steady tone, taking care to speak slowly and carefully in light of his visitor's obvious agitation.

'Yes, exactly. Yes.'

'So why didn't you come yesterday?'

'Well, you see…' he said and stopped. 'Of course I should have come yesterday, but I wanted to be certain. I wanted to make sure before I went off and got myself into trouble. I wanted to be sure my boy hadn't taken it. He said he hadn't.' Ingólfur looked up suddenly, a look of panic warping his features. 'Oh! Please don't misunderstand me. My son has no interest in guns, and … Well, the truth is that it's partly my fault. I kept it in an unlocked garage.' He hung his head for a moment, but lifted it to look straight into Ari Thór's eyes before continuing. 'But I can't keep quiet any longer, especially if it turns out the poor man was shot with my gun.'

'I expect there'll be some questions to answer later about how the gun was stored,' Ari Thór said. 'But we won't worry about that for the moment. You're saying that your son denied taking the weapon?'

'That's right.'

'And you believe him?'

'What? Yes, yes, of course I do.'

'And you? I don't suppose you had anything to do with the shooting?'

The words were almost a careless remark, but Ingólfur didn't seem to register Ari Thór's tone.

'What? No! What do you mean? I don't know the man at all. You think that I did it, tried to kill him?'

'I didn't say that. Who else lives with you? Is it a detached house?'

'It's detached. My wife and I live there, and so does our son. He's finishing college in the spring. He's in some of my classes, and he's doing all right…' He looked puzzled by the direction the conversation was taking. 'But about the gun, can you keep it out of the newspapers?'

'We don't make a habit of telling the newspapers about every lead.'

'No, I mean, can you keep me out of it? It's the boy I'm thinking of, so he doesn't get bullied at school,' he said. Either he was a good actor, or he was genuinely deeply distressed.

'Did many people know there was a gun in your garage? Is the garage part of the house? Have you noticed anyone suspicious hanging around?'

Ingólfur didn't seem to be sure which question to answer first.

'Well, no. No. The garage is next to the house, and I didn't notice anything. Not that it would be a problem to sneak in there, but people don't do that kind of thing in Siglufjördur. People leave you alone.'

'Most of the time, yes.'

Times were undeniably changing and the town was no longer quite as peaceful as it had been in the past. When Ari Thór had first arrived, Tómas told him that nothing ever happened in Siglufjördur, but now the new tunnel had brought the town closer to the main roads and it was starting to become busier. There were more visitors, more traffic. In some ways this was a positive development, but it was also clear that outsiders brought more than just a boost to the tourist industry.

'What were those last questions again?'

'Who knew you kept the shotgun there?'

'It wasn't a secret. Loads of people, I imagine. I'm in a hunting club and all the boys know I have a shotgun, but none of them would do anything like that; shoot a cop, I mean.'

Ari Thór gave him a pen and paper and asked him to write down the names of the hunting club members. When Ingólfur gave the page back there were five names on the list.

'And ammunition? Was that kept in the garage as well?'

Ingólfur hesitated and looked at his feet. Ari Thór wondered, was he going to tell the truth?

'Well, I think it was. Not always. But this time the shells were in the garage.'

'And are any of them missing?'

'I don't really know. I'm not sure how many were there to start with.'

Ari Thór nodded, and sat silently, hoping that Ingólfur might say something else.

'Keep quiet about this for the moment,' Ari Thór said, finally. On occasion, he found himself behaving just like Tómas, in both word and deed.

'Well, yeah. Yes.'

'I'll ask my colleague and the technical team to pay you a visit.'

'Isn't it illegal to keep it like that, in an unlocked garage? With the shells as well?' Ingólfur looked worried, as if regretting having turned himself in. 'Can't we just say the garage was locked and the thief broke in?'

'Absolutely not.'

If Ingólfur's shotgun *had* been used, was this his way of trying to avoid suspicion…? Coming to the police on his own initiative, playing the shocked and worried citizen.

For a moment Ari Thór wondered if he sat face to face with the killer.

The nights are the hardest. Sometimes I can get to sleep, but mostly I lie awake and listen to the 'silence'. There's never really silence here, of course, just different levels of sound. Underneath everything there's a hum and I don't know where it comes from; maybe from the lights or the radiators or the wires running through the walls of this sprawling hospital. I just know that the hum can drive you insane. There are other sounds in the silence, people going in and out, even muted chatter. Doors open and close, some people are free to come and go. Then there's the sound of traffic, car horns out there, on the other side of the windows, where normal people live and are free to do as they please.

The door to my room can be closed at night now. I'm apparently no longer a danger to myself. It's a little lonely not having someone on duty outside my door. Can you miss being under surveillance? Can you miss having a public employee sitting there watching you, watching your every move?

I try to remind myself that I'm now here of my own free will. Being free is wonderful, even though there can be an uncomfortable burden of responsibility that goes with it. There's so much that has to be decided, not least which direction I should take in my life. I don't know yet where life will lead me, still less how I'm supposed to behave around other people. Maybe that's what is making me so anxious. And maybe that's the reason for the clumsy suicide attempt. I like writing those words — suicide attempt. A man should take responsibility for his actions. That's what I was brought up to believe and that's how I'd prefer to live. That's definitely what Dad preached, although he didn't always follow his own advice.

It's stale and airless in here, especially at night. There is a pervading smell, some hospital odour that's difficult to describe. Should I try? It's slightly bitter, uncomfortable … it smells of hopelessness, really, and the medication that creates it.

The tune comes back to me sometimes, the melody. There's so much *going on in my head, thoughts bouncing back and forth, getting in each others' way, worries, tension, guilt. There's not much joy there.*

I often think of Hanna and of everything that went wrong between us. Or rather, what went wrong with me. It had all started so well and I was sure she was in love. I remember the first time we met, at school. We were the same age, but she was so much more mature. And I remember the last time I saw her, in tears, angry and betrayed. There was hatred in her eyes. That's how I know she won't be visiting me and I will probably never see her again unless by some coincidence, in which case I'll only be able to hang my head in shame and try to smile through it. I'm sorry. I couldn't help myself. My temper got the better of me. And she'll look away and cross the street to avoid me.

I couldn't help myself.

My temper got the better of me

Is that what really happened?

I'm searching for the answer to that question.

And the answer scares me.

17

Was that too far? Did I go too far?

It was all Elín could think about on her way up to the ski lodge high in the valley. She took pride in her work and was annoyed that she'd put herself in this position. She'd never be able to concentrate on her meeting with the managers of the ski slopes. Although she knew that she was hard working and clever, she was also aware that the real reason she had this job was down to Gunnar, and she owed him for that. He had appointed her without advertising the position, despite her sketchy experience and her unfinished master's degree.

Of course she *had* crossed a line. However you wanted to look at it, Gunnar was a married man, in name at least, an old and valued friend, a colleague, and, yes, on top of that he was her boss. Yet she had still allowed herself to go a step too far.

But the ends would more than justify the means. She was determined to give it a go, to try to steal Gunnar from his wife. The marriage had clearly come to an end, even if Gunnar and his wife weren't ready to admit it. Elín was in the best position to see the truth. She had been attracted to Gunnar for as long as she had known him, but never thought that she would have a chance – until now. The marriage coming apart at the seams, his wife far away, and the two of them, Elín and Gunnar, in exile in this little town beneath the towering mountains in the north of Iceland. It couldn't get any better than that.

She looked up at the mountains on her way up the valley, most of them white-covered even though the ski slopes wouldn't be open for a while yet. The mountains encircling Siglufjördur always seemed to be white, even at the height of summer when remnants of the winter snowfall still clung to the peaks. She had been told that soon, around the middle of November, the sun would disappear behind the mountains for its long winter break and it wouldn't return until late January, when the town would celebrate with solar coffee and pancakes. Elín still found it odd to contemplate complete, round-the-clock darkness. Even though the winter sun in the south was neither bright nor high in the sky, she still found it difficult to imagine living in a place where the sun simply went away, hiding behind the mountains that enclosed the small town on three sides. To Elin it was unsettling, almost eerie and threatening. But the townspeople seemed to take it in their stride.

Her thoughts flashed back to Gunnar, and she felt disgruntled. It had always been her intention to give their deepening friendship a nudge in the right direction, but had she been too hasty? She didn't want to let this opportunity slip through her fingers, though. Gunnar was vulnerable right now, for a variety of reasons, and not least because he was now caught up in this police investigation, alone and with no support, far from his family. Of course the man needed someone to lean on. It made perfect sense that she should be there for him; she'd been a family friend for years and even knew his wife well enough. There had always been a level of polite suspicion between them, and if she and Gunnar were to form a relationship, there would certainly be some venom spat from Norway. Hopefully the howls of fury would be muted somewhere over the ocean. Elín lifted her chin determinedly. She wasn't going to let Gunnar get away. A decent man, reliable, handsome, ambitious, and the mayor; they got on so well together. They had known each other for a long time and the prospect of a possible romance had always loomed in the air, just within reach.

She deserved a good man, and she'd waited long enough for someone she could really love. Previously, she always seemed to go for the wrong sort – men who were difficult, dangerous, even downright cruel. She'd loved Gunnar from afar, and knew he was a man who would treat her well. The job he'd offered appeared out of nowhere, but it was highly appreciated. She had been stuck in a block of flats in Kópavogur, with a man she couldn't stand, from whom she didn't dare walk away.

They had met at a nightspot in Kópavogur, where her college reunion had been taking place. He hadn't been to college with the rest of them, but crashed the party and ended up at a table with Elín and her friend. Although there was something vaguely sinister about him, he came across well. And she had to admit to herself that it was precisely that hint of danger that had pressed all of her buttons. They went home together, to his place. The violence didn't start right away, not until she had moved in, by which time he had won her trust, caught her in his net and aroused in her some strong feelings for him, more than just affection even if it wasn't quite love. It was when they disagreed that he started to use his fists to drive home his point of view, although he always apologised profusely later on. Of course she should have walked out there and then, that first time, but she always fell into the same trap, struggling to leave men like this, to whom she couldn't help being drawn.

Valberg hadn't looked the violent type, in fact, he held down a good job at a small advertising agency and was well liked there, a cheerful, positive character with plenty of friends. But the glint she had seen in his eye that first night, that undefinable but immediate sense of danger that he exuded and which drew her to him had turned out to be an indication of worse to come, a wisp of smoke from a raging fire within.

It reached the point that she didn't dare leave. The growing violence was soon accompanied by threats, as well as a deep jealousy. *I'll kill you if you go.* And she was sure that he would keep his promise. Of course she should have left, and gone straight to the police. But it wasn't that easy. Where would she go? She didn't trust the police to protect her and a charge of threatening behaviour wouldn't be much of a deterrent. On top of that, it would be her word against his. He was careful to cover his tracks; no written threats, no angry text messages. He was a disturbingly clever character.

She hadn't heard from Gunnar for a while when she received his call to offer her a job. She had hesitated for a moment, but quickly realised that this was her escape route. She could get away from Valberg, away to a place that felt like the other side of the world. Of course she had known of Siglufjördur, but she had never been there and it was off the beaten track in more ways than one. She disappeared while Valberg was at work. It didn't cross her mind to say goodbye to him. She changed her phone number and made sure that she kept her registered residence in Reykjavík, so he wouldn't be able to track her down. To be entirely sure that she couldn't be found, Elín gave herself a brand-new surname to go with the new job. Elín Einarsdóttir became the deputy mayor, Elín Reyndal, an unofficial name change, and something to ensure that Valberg would never find her. Reyndal was an old family name that had belonged to her mother's family, a name that no close relative used.

Elín was aware that it was only a temporary solution.

Almost every night she awoke, bathed in sweat after some unpleasantly realistic nightmare in which Valberg appeared in Siglufjördur – or she was still in Kópavogur, subject to his violence, his twitching rage, his threats. She escaped her dreams to hide in her new reality, but she woke every day with a deep nausea and an overwhelming fear that it was only a question of time before he caught up with her. She knew that time would weaken his power over her, and make it less likely that he would seek her out and carry out his threats, but she was still afraid. She had no desire to spend her life on the run, and the secrets she buried were a constant threat to her ability to concentrate, to do her job. Too many times she'd thought she'd seen Valberg out of the corner of her eye, an unsettling experience that proved simply to be a mirage, the product of her fearful imagination.

She had told Gunnar some of the story, but not all of it. She toned it down, made light of her fear. But he knew that she was in hiding and did his best to help her. They had been close friends and confidantes in the past, close enough to share secrets.

'Why didn't you tell me before?' was the first question he asked when she told him how things had been. 'You should have called me.'

She didn't even try to make excuses. That wasn't her style, and anyway, she didn't owe him any apologies. They were good friends, but it went no further than that.

'You think we can make this work out in Siglufjördur?' she asked instead. 'I'd like to move on and the job sounds good to me.'

Everything had worked out, right up until the police came knocking on Gunnar's door, asking about the shooting. Or, rather, it had started with Herjólfur's call to Gunnar the night before the shooting. That triggered a chain of events to which she could see no end.

I met Dr Helgi, briefly today, and about time.

He didn't have much to say, but at least he seemed to remember who I am. I'm probably one of the youngest inmates here and although I don't cast a long shadow, keeping to myself and sticking to the corners, my father is the type of character nobody easily forgets. He has an authority about him. He's burly and strong, much like me, unfortunately.

Dad is decisive and he's arrogant, the type who always gets his way. The type nobody wants to stand up to.

The doctor prescribed some medication for me and I thanked him for it, almost as though I had a choice in the matter. I waited for him to offer me a seat, and to lean back in his chair so we could talk through the past and the future, the reasons for my being here and how I can make a recovery.

But there was no such discussion. He prompted me to leave, first with a glance and then, as I made no move to be on my way, with a wave of his hand. That was enough.

I start on this course of medication right away. It takes two weeks for the medication to start to work, and by then Dad should be able to see my progress. I'll be able to come out of this place a better man, promising never to do it again, just as little children do. Little children...

18

'Isn't this beautiful?' Tómas asked as they approached the ski lodge on the landward side of the town, the encircling snow-capped mountains picture perfect. As they drove up the hills, then into the valley, everything was more or less covered in snow, an early reminder that the Christmas season would soon commence.

Ari Thór smiled. 'You're missing Siglufjördur already?'

'Already? I was missing the place the same day we moved south.'

'Not ready to come back?' Ari Thór asked cautiously.

There was a heavy silence. 'Have you been over the mountain pass at Skardur?' he asked, as if he hadn't heard Ari Thór's question.

Ari Thór found himself looking up towards the old mountain road that had once been Siglufjördur's only link with the outside world, until the first tunnel had been opened in the sixties.

'I have to admit that I haven't,' he said with regret. The road was only open at the height of summer and it was clear that there would be no chance of going that way at the moment. 'I'll do it in the summer. I'll make time to go up there.'

'It can be dangerous in the summer as well,' Tómas said with a thoughtful look on his face as they arrived at their destination. 'I was stuck there once on a school trip, when I was only a child. It was summer, so we weren't all that warmly dressed, and halfway across, right at the top, a blinding snowstorm came down and the bus got stuck. We were terrified, and the weather got worse and worse. I remember it as if it were yesterday – it's the kind of experience that never leaves you. We were up there until past nightfall and they had to send the rescue teams out. Everyone who had something with four-wheel drive took part in the rescue, and the children had to be carried down, very slowly. You could see nothing but snow, not a thing. So we held hands in a little group and followed the grown-ups.'

There was a faraway look in his eyes, as if he was still there.

'I was at the back of the group and all of a sudden I lost my grip on the boy in front of me. The group kept going, even thought the boy tried to call out. I shouted, and then started to cry, but nobody heard me. But that boy wouldn't give up, and he pulled himself away from the line. That's when the others finally stopped. I was so cold, stiff with exhaustion and fear, and I'd stubbed my toes on a rock. If it wasn't for him … if he hadn't stopped…' Tómas turned to look at Ari Thór, something close to tears blurring his bright eyes. 'You know who he was, that boy? The one who risked being lost so he could help me?'

Ari Thór shook his head.

'That was Addi. Addi Gunna, my cousin. Everyone has a redeeming quality, Ari Thór. Even Addi,' he said in his habitually thoughtful way. 'And most of us have a darker side that not many people get to see.'

Tómas paused again. He had already described his second visit to Addi Gunna, and it seemed that no new information had emerged. He sounded like he was apologising for his cousin, pointing out his innate goodness as if to counter the fact that he was now embroiled in activities that were more than suspect. He looked over at Ari Thór, who nodded his understanding.

'I had a visitor myself,' said Ari Thór, and told him about the college teacher's lost shotgun.

Tómas raised an eyebrow. The case was definitely moving on.

Information on calls to and from the mayor's mobile phone were coming in rapidly, and it turned out that the mayor had been in unusually frequent communication with the deputy mayor, a woman who called herself Elín Reyndal, but whose name was actually Elín Einarsdóttir, according to the national register. The mayor had called her immediately after the police's unannounced visit.

'There's something fishy there,' Tómas had whispered, when they had arrived at the municipal offices and asked for Elín. They learned that she had gone to attend a meeting up in the valley, at the lodge on the ski slopes. Conscious that he needed to maintain a good relationship with the local authority once the investigation was over, Ari Thór had suggested they come back the next day to talk to her, but Tómas wouldn't hear of it. When this usually reserved man had the bit between his teeth, there was no hope of persuading him to change his mind.

'No. We'll go now. And we won't call ahead to let her know we're on the way. Sometimes catching people off guard brings you a windfall.'

Tables and chairs had been arranged in rows inside the ski lodge, although only three people were to be seen, a man and two women. The wall of shelves behind them was filled with ski boots and helmets, all ready for the coming winter. They looked up as the two police officers walked in. Ari Thór recognised Elín immediately, and knew that the man and woman she was sitting opposite were the couple who ran the ski slopes. They were a young and energetic pair with ambitious ideas for the area that the locals modestly referred to as the Siglufjördur Alps.

It was clear from the look on Elín's face that she had expected this visit, but there was no hint of nerves. She seemed prepared, almost defiant, looking from one of her companions to the other as she waited for the officers to state their business. It seemed that Tómas had been right. If she was expecting them, then she must have something to say – or something to hide. It had probably been the right decision not to put off this conversation for too long.

'Good afternoon,' Ari Thór offered, his words directed at Elín. 'We need a word with you. Do you have a moment?'

The ski couple's eyes widened, as if they were witnessing a major event being played out in real time on television.

Elín sat still, looked firmly at Ari Thór, refusing to be intimidated.

'I'm in a meeting. Can this wait?'

'No,' Ari Thór replied sharply, immediately irritated by her attitude.

She stood up quickly. 'We can talk outside.'

He would have preferred to have remained inside the ski lodge to talk to her. It was cosy inside and Ari Thór's thoughts had again moved to the impending winter. This warm mountain hut would be a welcome refuge when the snow began to fall in earnest. And it was already growing increasingly cold outside, the temperatures definitely descending below zero.

They went outside and Elín followed. It was early afternoon and dusk was approaching; the cold was piercing. It was a beautiful day, but one best enjoyed from behind a window. A brooding silence settled over the valley. It seemed so empty, the ski lift motionless, nobody skiing, no activity anywhere.

'Shall we sit in the car?' Tómas asked.

'Not unless I'm being arrested,' Elín replied, appearing to be fully in control. 'I'm fine out here. Are you gentlemen feeling the cold?' she added, looking first at Ari Thór and then at Tómas.

'Elín Reyndal,' Tómas said. 'Or Elín Einarsdóttir?'

'Either will work,' she said, drawing her lips together in a tight line.

'Is there a particular reason why you're not using your given name? And why your legal residence is registered down south?'

'Reyndal is an old and perfectly good family name. I don't see any reason why I shouldn't use it if I feel like it.'

'Nobody's implying that you shouldn't,' Tómas said. 'It's just curious.'

'Whatever you say.'

'And the legal residence, I'd have thought you would be registered here in Siglufjördur. You live here permanently, don't you?'

'That's not certain yet. I haven't been here long,' she said coolly. 'But since you ask, I plan to change it. I don't suppose two police officers came up here to ask about an incorrectly registered address?' she asked, a cold look on her face.

'What kind of relationship do you have with the mayor, Gunnar Gunnarsson?' Tómas asked.

'I work for him.'

'Have you known him long?' Ari Thór broke in.

'We were at school together,' she said. It seemed she was going to offer little beyond the bare facts.

'Close friends?'

She hesitated at last. 'Friends, yes. Nothing more.'

'And is that how you got the job?'

'Just what are you insinuating?'

Now it was Ari Thór's turn to hesitate, concerned that he might be on thin ice. 'Well, it seems like he wanted to employ someone he knew.'

'He knows me well enough to realise that I'm trustworthy. That's all there is to it.'

She glanced at her watch and then at her car. 'I have to go. And I still don't see why you had to drag me away from a meeting.'

'You have plenty to say to each other, you and Gunnar,' Tómas said calmly, ignoring her growing agitation.

'Of course we talk to each other.'

'On the phone? Every morning and evening?' he asked, his statement becoming a question.

Elín hesitated again. The hint of red that flushed her cheeks could have been the cold.

'We sometimes talk,' she said.

'More than sometimes, I'd say, not that I have a precise figure for all the phone calls yet.'

'What the hell do you mean? Have you been tapping my phone?'

Tómas grinned. 'Nothing as serious as that, and if we were, I'd hardly tell you. We don't make that kind of information public. All I can tell you is that we have a record of calls to and from Gunnar's phone. Your name comes up frequently.'

She seemed taken aback and Ari Thór started to suspect that her tough exterior might not be so impenetrable after all.

She gave herself a moment to think. 'I don't see quite where this is going. I have no obligation to explain myself and my conversations with Gunnar. And before you ask, I'm not sleeping with him.'

'I wasn't going to ask,' Tómas said. 'The other day we paid Gunnar a visit and hauled him gently over the coals…'

Ari Thór instinctively looked sideways, as if he wanted to say 'your words, not mine'.

Elín waited in silence.

'And you know what the first thing he did was once the interrog– meeting … was finished?' Tómas asked.

Elín shook her head.

'He called you.' There was a short silence before Tómas contin-ued. 'Why was that? What did he need to tell you?'

'Tell me?' she demanded, buying herself a moment. 'We were discussing planning issues.'

The defiant front was starting to crumble and Ari Thór's first thought was that this was bad lying; she was probably saying the first thing that entered her mind.

'Planning for the ski area?' he asked with pointed courtesy.

'What? I don't remember. It could well have been.'

She looked at her watch again.

'Were you in contact with Herjólfur?' Tómas asked, apparently in no hurry to bring the conversation to an end, despite the bitter cold. This was a wonderful area to visit in summertime, a place where temperatures could reach very high figures on a sunny day, but on a day like this, it made no sense to stand still and be tortured by the chill.

Ari Thór slipped away, as inconspicuously as he could. Once he was sitting in the patrol car, he called the mayor's mobile number and Gunnar answered after a couple of rings.

'Yes? Hello?'

It was clear he hadn't realised who was calling.

'Hello, this is Ari Thór from the police. Am I interrupting anything?'

'No, not at all. I've just got home.'

A little early in the day for the mayor to be going home, Ari Thór thought.

'After we came to see you the other day, Tómas and I…'

'Yes … of course, yes,' Gunnar broke in.

'You called your colleague, Elín.' There was a silence on the other end of the line, and Ari Thór decided to let it become a long one, striking while the iron was at its hottest. After a few more moments of silence, he added, 'Why did you do that?'

'Why did I do that?'

'Was there something you wanted to warn her about?' Ari Thór asked, taking care to keep the same measured tone.

'No, of course not. No. I, er … I just wanted just let her know that the police had been to see me about the investigation, just in case anyone might be asking. So we could respond correctly.'

Ari Thór could hear Gunnar's short, sharp breathing down the line. He or Elín was lying, or maybe they both were. It had been a smart move on Tómas's part to apply for the phone records, even though there had not been strong grounds to back up the request.

'I'm sorry, but I'm not entirely sure I understand you,' Ari Thór said courteously. 'Would you have had to respond? Is she also the mayor's press officer?'

'Well, no. Not at all. But we work closely together. I took her on because I've known her for a long time and I was confident that I could trust her. I could say that she's my right hand,' Gunnar said, his voice taking a sharper edge. 'How on earth did you know about that call? Not that I have anything to hide…'

'We have a list of the calls made to and from your phone.'

'What? Is that something you have access to?'

'No, we applied for a warrant.'

'A warrant?'

'That's right. So we would have all the facts, because you and Herjólfur had spoken so shortly before he was shot.'

'Were you looking into just *my* calls or others as well?' he asked and Ari Thór could detect a combination of anger and fear in his voice.

'I'm afraid I can't answer that. I'm sure you understand.'

Ari Thór saw that Tómas was making his way back to the car, his conversation with Elín over.

'I have to go, Gunnar. Thanks for your time,' Ari Thór said, and hung up.

'A chat with the mayor?' Tómas asked, the moment he was behind the wheel. It was an old habit for Tómas to do all the driving.

Ari Thór nodded.

'Excellent, my boy. Excellent. And what did he say?'

'Not the same as Elín.'

'It gets better and better. In fact, this is going to be very interesting.' Tómas started the car, a smile behind the thoughtful look on his face. They were on to something, and Ari Thór was quite sure that things were not going to end well for the mayor of Siglufjördur.

I wrote nothing yesterday.

The whole day was spent lying in bed.

It'll make you feel better, Dr Helgi had said. That was one of the few things he had to say before he dismissed me from his office.

What a load of shit! I've never felt worse. These pills aren't doing me any good. Quite the opposite. I'm nothing like my normal self. I sleep worse than before and my mouth is dry all the time. You're supposed to be patient with these drugs and 'work with your medication', or so the staff keeps reminding me.

It's midday. Actually I don't have a watch so I don't know exactly what the time is, but we've just been called to lunch. That means it's midday in this little community. I'm not going, I don't feel up to it.

It'll pass, or so I'm told, all these side-effects and teething problems that are part of my new relationship with medication.

Nobody needs a watch here. Time passes in a rhythm dictated by an organised timetable; breakfast, morning meeting, lunch, afternoon coffee, dinner. Then it all starts again the next day. The fucking monotony of it would drive a sane man crazy, although I have to concede that there is something soothing about it all. Before, I used to dread each new day, not knowing what it might bring, but that feeling is starting to fade away now. Just like I am.

19

Kristín was nowhere to be seen when Ari Thór arrived home at dinner time, and he assumed she must be upstairs putting Stefnir to bed. He had brought a pizza home with him, but saw as soon he went into the kitchen that Kristín and Stefnir had already had fish. There were no leftovers for him in the fridge, which was possibly a silent rebuke for having been away from his family so often since the investigation had begun. Or maybe Kristín had simply not expected him to be home for dinner.

He would have liked to have crept up the stairs to take a peek at them, but knew that Kristín would take a dim view of an interruption while she was getting the boy off to sleep. He was probably better off in the kitchen with the pizza while it was still warm. Siglufjördur's police force didn't live on doughnuts. The mainstay of their diet was pizza, as well as those cinnamon buns that the local bakery did so well.

Ari Thór had missed the evening news on television and he wasn't sorry. He had already seen and heard enough news reports speculating the specifics of the attack. An armed assault on a police officer was a major story, unprecedented in the history of the small island, so there wasn't much else in the news, even though the investigation had made little appreciable progress. He had no need to listen to journalists telling him what he already knew, that the case was still unresolved. They had probably found the owner of the shotgun, Ingólfur the teacher – or he'd found them. The forensic team had searched Ingólfur's garage without discovering anything that might be relevant to the case. Ari Thór found Ingólfur's story plausible and the gun had presumably been stolen. It seemed that the assault weapon was the same type of gun, but a match would not be possible until the shotgun itself was found.

His neighbours had been interviewed to find out if anyone had seen anything, but nothing had emerged. The case remained shrouded in darkness. Ingólfur would have to be considered a suspect, but Ari Thór found it difficult to imagine that he could be guilty of anything other than carelessness.

The police had not yet made this new angle of the investigation public, and deep inside he hoped that Ingólfur could be shielded from the spotlight, although that was probably unlikely. The forensic team's investigation of his garage in broad daylight would certainly not have escaped notice, and that kind of gossip would spread like wildfire in the small community. It wouldn't be long before hungry journalists would be sniffing at the trail.

Seeking some company to go with his pizza, he finally switched on the television only to find a studio debate on gun ownership taking place, a subject that rarely attracted any attention in Iceland. It wasn't difficult to work out what had prompted the discussion.

'There are sixty thousand registered firearms in Iceland,' said one of the panel members. 'Sixty thousand! That means every fifth Icelander has a weapon, and if we only take into consideration the adult population, gun ownership is much higher. A few years ago a survey showed that Iceland has the fifteenth-highest level of gun ownership worldwide per capita. Fifteenth! Chances are these figures are much lower than the reality, too.'

A society of hunters, Ari Thór thought to himself.

'Per capita,' someone else said, interrupting the debate on the screen. 'You can get all kinds of weird and wonderful numbers per capita…'

'Excuse me?' The first one squawked. 'In fifteenth place. Going by those figures, we must have ninety thousand firearms. What on earth do we need all those guns for? Isn't it about time the rules were tightened up? And what comes next? Arming the police? It seems that everyone except the police has access to firearms.'

Ari Thór was quietly enjoying the argument, when a loud knock at the door shattered his peaceful meal. He was startled. Putting down his half-eaten slice of pizza, he stood up, gripped by a feeling of unease that he did his best to ignore. He wasn't expecting anyone and it was most unlike Tómas to call unannounced.

He glanced at his phone to see if anyone had tried to contact him, and to make sure he hadn't accidentally turned it off or silenced it, but that was not the case. There was not really any reason to be concerned by an unannounced caller, not in Siglufjördur. A more peaceful spot could hardly be imagined. This was a place where, on occasions, the forces of nature were to be feared, but not the neighbours. But now someone had shot one of the town's two police officers at close range. The remaining police officer was Ari Thór. Was there someone with a grudge against the police? Was Herjólfur just the first victim?

The knock was repeated, loud and determined.

A moment later there was a bang on the ceiling above. The old house was built of wood and sound carried well throughout it. Kristín had undoubtedly heard Ari Thór come home and then the knocking on the front door. Her bang on the floor was a clear instruction for him to answer the door promptly while she was getting Stefnir to sleep.

Ari Thór hurried to the hallway.

The lightbulb by the front door needed replacing so he peered into the darkness to see the face of someone he recognised but had never spoken to. Ottó N. Níelsson stood there, Siglufjördur's newly elected town councillor, born and raised in the town, and recently returned to his home turf after many years in Reykjavík.

'Good evening, Ari Thór,' he said in a deep bass voice, before Ari Thór could open his mouth. 'I hope I'm not intruding? I'd appreciate a word with you.'

As he had taken the trouble to visit after dark, the errand had to be something urgent.

'Yes, won't you come in?'

'That would be appreciated. Much appreciated,' Ottó said, carefully wiping non-existent mud from his shoes onto the mat before coming inside and following Ari Thór into the living room. Ottó made himself comfortable in the middle of the sofa. Ari Thór found it awkward having this stranger call on him so late in the day and was relieved that Kristín was busy upstairs.

Ari Thór knew a little of Ottó's background. He was a high-profile member of Reykjavík's business community and had done very well for himself with the acquisition of the remnants of a debt-laden car dealership just when demand for new vehicles had dropped to virtually zero. According to rumour, he had been able to sell the company at a considerable profit a few years later once the economy had begun to recover from the financial crash. He had moved back to Siglufjördur, stood in the municipal elections and had been elected. He was also believed to have applied pressure for Gunnar Gunnarsson to be appointed mayor; Gunnar being a close friend of his, but an outsider with little experience.

Ari Thór sat and waited for his visitor to get to the point.

'How's the investigation going?' Ottó asked, his deep voice appearing to well up from the depths of his torso. His gaze didn't waver from Ari Thór's face and it was obvious that something more than simple curiosity had brought him.

'Reasonably well,' Ari Thór answered, keeping his answer short. Ottó sat silently. 'Of course, I'm not at liberty to discuss details,' he said to break the silence.

'Exactly. Of course,' Ottó said.

'Would you like a cup of coffee?' Ari Thór asked, hoping that he would say no.

'Not for me, but thanks all the same. I'm not stopping.' He leaned forward. 'You've been speaking to Gunnar, and more than once, or so I understand. Or interrogating him, if that's the word…'

'I can't confirm…' Ari Thór began, before Ottó interrupted.

'Gunnar told me himself, so there's no need for you to confirm anything. And earlier today you were pestering the deputy mayor,

Elín Reyndal,' he said before Ari Thór could reply. Ottó laid particular emphasis on the word 'pestering'.

'As I told you, I'm not in a position to discuss details of the case…'

'Fine, fine. You and Tómas have spoken to both Gunnar and Elín, and I can't for the life of me understand why. I know, or at least I'm sure enough, that this was Tómas's doing. I remember him from the old days. He's pushy, in his own way. He moves south, gets a smart promotion and then there's this opportunity to run the investigation here. Of course the old boy's going to want to make his presence felt. That's what I'm saying, Ari Thór … I mean that I'm not blaming you for any of this.'

He paused and continued.

'I decided I needed a quiet word with you. With you, not Tómas. I can trust you and I know you're a local, or almost a local now, practically part of the landscape. But Tómas has moved away and isn't likely to be coming back. Do you really believe the mayor could have attempted to murder a police inspector? What do you think?' He stared hard at Ari Thór. 'Or the deputy mayor? Be serious now.'

Ari Thór stood up and smiled. He hadn't been called a local in Siglufjördur before, and was certain that Ottó was only doing it now because he needed a favour.

'I'm afraid I can't discuss this with you and I hope you understand. The investigation is at a very sensitive stage. You can imagine how it would look if word were to get out that you were sitting here and I was giving you details of the case.'

Ottó stood up as well.

'Why should word get out?'

Ari Thór extended a hand.

'It's good to meet you, Ottó, and thank you for stopping by. There's no need for concern because the investigation is in capable hands and I expect the case will be resolved in the next couple of days.'

'It will be if you stop wasting time on irrelevant stuff. It looks bad for everyone, Ari Thór, if word gets out that the police are repeatedly

interrogating senior municipal officials … and not just the mayor,'
Ottó said, his voice gaining volume, the threat clear.

Ari Thór showed his visitor to the door, outwardly maintaining
his composure despite the thoughts now swirling in his mind.

When Ottó had gone, Ari Thór stood for a while in the hall and
reflected upon their encounter. Had he been too courteous, considering the circumstances? Or maybe too discourteous?

His gut feeling was that neither Gunnar nor Elín had anything to
do with the shooting, and maybe he and Tómas had applied more
pressure than was warranted in exploring those avenues. At the heart
of the matter was the fact that once the investigation had been con-
cluded, he would have to continue to live in this close little community while Tómas returned to his post in the south. He was in
no position to put his job or his family at risk, nor the prospect of a
promotion if Herjólfur didn't make it. Ari Thór would have to take
his next steps very, very carefully.

I had a long talk with the nurse today. This wasn't because I get any particular satisfaction from talking to her, but because, unlike the doctor, she can actually be bothered to listen to me.

Bothered to listen? Well ... she listened, at least, but it has to be remembered that she gets paid for looking after the inmates. I tried to turn on the charm, told her she was the only one working here who has any sense. I think she's actually a bit stupid, but what the hell? She listened.

I didn't go so far as to tell her the whole story from the start, why I'm the way I am, but I tried to get her to understand that the medication is having a terrible effect and it's really making things worse. I told her that I don't have to be here, but with things as they are at the moment, I'll allow myself to be led by the doctors. All I need is different medication.

She promised to do her best, said that Dr Helgi wouldn't be back for a while, but that he could be reached in an emergency. Maybe that's what we need. An emergency.

20

Ari Thór was up and about early. He felt much better physically than he had over the last few days, as he was finally gaining the upper hand over the flu that had plagued him. Kristín's odd behaviour was however still cause for concern, but he needed to be able to focus on the investigation.

Ottó's visit had preyed on his mind all evening, but he had been able to get to sleep easily. He and Kristín were woken by Stefnir at six, but the little boy was persuaded to close his eyes again. With a day off ahead of her, Kristín settled back to sleep, but Ari Thór remained awake, his mind turning over the facts of a case that was evolving in directions that were increasingly interesting. He had mentioned to Tómas that he was interested in speaking to the elderly lady who knew the dark history of the house where Herjólfur had been shot. Her name was Jódís, the sister of the man who had been in the house with the twin brothers Baldur and Börkur when Baldur had lost his life, tumbling from the balcony almost half a century ago.

It had been agreed that the best time to meet her would be over morning coffee at the church hall.

'It's a custom that started with the Reverend Eggert,' said Tómas, 'opening the hall up every weekday morning at seven and offering coffee. My cousin's a regular there, and I hear Jódís is as well.'

It was undoubtedly going to be a long, tough day, so it would be good to start with a relaxed chat, making the most of the morning before the phone calls started, the media woke up and Tómas started issuing instructions.

Ari Thór stepped outside into a cold northerly breeze. The

distance to the church was so short it made no sense to drive. It had snowed during the night, and the temperature was hovering below zero, cold enough to give the pavements a crispness underfoot, with a glistening aura of frost enveloping the town. There was a sharp wind, an indication of the real winter, lurking behind the corner. Ari Thór had seen mild winters in Reykjavík, but here in Siglufjördur the concept of a mild winter was unheard of.

Ari Thór walked briskly up the church steps and went upstairs to the long room that served as the church hall, feeling his strength returning.

He had made a point of wearing civilian clothing, as this wasn't exactly a police matter and uniform would hardly have been appropriate under the circumstances. But there was no chance of his becoming lost in the throng. In one corner sat a group of pensioners. As Ari Thór appeared, the average age of those present dropped significantly, and the whole group fell silent. The Reverend Eggert was nowhere to be seen, but one of the guests, a man who looked to be well into his eighties, spoke for them all.

'Good morning. Would you like to join us?'

Not knowing Jódís by sight, he decided to take a shot in the dark.

'Thank you. I don't want to interrupt, but I'm hoping to find Jódís.'

One of the women at the table looked up. 'I've finished my coffee and I'll be interested to know what you want with me, young man.' She stood up and extended a delicate, bony hand. 'I'm Jódís. And you are...?'

'Ari Thór,' he said, taking her hand. She was much shorter than he was, slightly hunched, her silver hair gathered into a bun, and she was wearing a neat dress in much the same colour.

'Let's sit ourselves down.' She pointed to a table a distance away from the group. 'Over there?'

'Fine.'

'Excellent.' They sat on either side of the table, the cloying smell of her perfume almost overwhelming, even from several feet away.

'I had been expecting you, or someone else.' She pressed her lips together in a prim smile.

'Me or someone else?'

'Yes. You're with the police, aren't you?' she asked, a sparkle in her eye. 'Aren't you going to ask me about the house?'

'Quite right,' Ari Thór said, taken by surprise.

'And what is it you want to know, if you don't mind me asking?'

'Well, I'm just curious about the history of the place.'

'And you think, young man, that the history of the house can shine a little light on the events of these past few days? That the past holds the key to today's mysteries?'

'You never know.'

'I must say I'm doubtful, but I won't avoid your questions. Not that I'm sure I'll have all the answers. I hope you understand.'

Ari Thór nodded. 'Of course. This is just an informal chat. Nothing official.'

'Then we're on the same page,' Jódís smiled. 'That's always a good way to start.'

'A man lost his life in the house approximately fifty years ago?'

'I think you know that as well as I do,' she said good-naturedly.

'And your brother was present when this happened?'

'That's right. His name was Jónmundur. We were Jónmundur and Jódís. He's long gone. I imagine you knew this before you came to find me. All three of them are gone: Jónmundur, Börkur and Baldur.'

'When did this happen, precisely? Around 1960, I was told.'

'The autumn of 1961, and that was a memorable year for plenty of reasons. It was one of the best herring years. We set a record that summer when we salted seventeen thousand barrels in one day. Seventeen thousand!' She smiled at the memory. 'I can say "we" because I was part of it. I don't suppose that you'll understand how important the herring was in those days.'

Ari Thór was too young to have remembered the herring era in Siglufjördur, but he had nevertheless read about it, and heard many herring tales after moving up north. Siglufjördur had been the biggest herring port in Iceland, and had multiplied in size when the herring fishery was at its peak. The first herring factory in the town had been built in the early twentieth century, and for a while herring was one of Iceland's most valuable exports. Everyone in town – men, women and children – took part when the fish were being landed; working in the factories, salting herring into barrels. There had been no shortage of money floating around, for the people of Siglufjör-dur as well as all the others who came into town to work in the fish business. Everyone had a role to play to make sure that the silver of the sea was turned into a valuable commodity. But then at the end of the 1960s, the herring had vanished, it left the northerly shores of Iceland. Today Siglufjördur was a completely different place, and although the herring years still held an important place in the mem-ories of the townspeople, it was difficult for a younger man and an outsider to understand fully the atmosphere of a bygone era.

'Did they all work in the herring?'

'Yes, certainly. Everyone did.'

'And was there a party that night when the incident occurred?'

'We didn't talk much about parties in those days. But they were good friends, Jónmundur and the twins, and they liked a dram or two when they got together. They were not temperance types, I can assure you.'

'And were they all together the night Börkur … I mean the night Baldur lost his life?' Ari Thór asked awkwardly, forced to admit to himself that he hadn't been sure which of the twins had fallen to his death.

'It was Baldur who fell,' Jódís said, a little coldly. 'Let's not get them mixed up.'

'Right,' he said, with the sudden feeling that he was seated in front of a strict teacher.

'They were there together, yes. I ask again, do you think these events from so long ago could have something to do with what the police is investigating now?'

'I understand if you'd prefer not to talk about it.'

'It was a tragedy. Nothing more.'

'An accident?'

'He fell from the balcony and didn't survive the fall.'

'Had he been drinking?'

She took her time and thought for a while before answering. 'I think the darkness was more of a factor than the drink, to be honest.'

'Did your brother witness it? Did he tell you anything about it?'

'That's two questions, young man. You're going to have to allow me to take them one at a time.'

'I'm sorry. Did your brother see anything?'

'No, he didn't.'

'Did he ever discuss that night with you? I mean, the events that took place that night?'

'No, he didn't.'

'Could it be possible that Börkur might have pushed Baldur off?' Ari Thór asked. *Börkur or Jónmundur*, he had wanted to ask, but was reluctant to upset the old lady.

She leaned forward and placed her hand on Ari Thór's arm.

'Sometimes the truth needs to rest in peace,' she whispered and stood up. 'Thank you so much for the chat, Ari Thór. It was very pleasant to meet you. But let me think things over. Maybe it's time to blow the dust off a few old secrets. Maybe.'

Jódís walked away with slow, decisive steps to her friends in the corner. She did not look back.

⊕

After his conversation with Jódís, Ari Thór walked home to change into uniform before meeting Tómas at the station. It didn't feel quite as cold as before, but the wind was blowing as hard as ever from the north, as if to ensure that Ari Thór wouldn't forget where in the world he was. He looked to the skies and saw only dark clouds.

'It was strange, to say the least,' he told Tómas, after recounting Ottó's visit the previous evening. 'A veiled threat, or so it seemed to me. He was quite tactful about it, but it's like nothing I've ever encountered before.'

'You'll get used to it,' was the first thing Tómas said. 'I never got on with Ottó.'

'Do you know him well?'

'We know each other well enough, but I don't have any contact with him these days. He made a lot of money after the financial crash, some business deal or other, but he keeps his cash down south and that's something that causes ill-feeling up here.'

'What do you mean, he keeps his cash down south?'

'He's involved in some investment business down there but lives here. There are a lot of people who reckon he ought to be investing at home, but not a penny comes this way. He was always a skinflint, the old man, and that hasn't changed. He likes to live here and sees himself as a local bigshot now that he's a town councillor. He'll buy groceries in the Co-op, but that's as far as it goes. Or so they say. But the fly in the ointment will be the news that emerged this morning. Ottó won't be impressed.'

'What news?'

'On the net, the news article about Elín.'

'Elín?' Ari Thór asked in confusion.

'Someone saw us up in the ski lodge yesterday and there's a gossip piece about the Siglufjördur deputy mayor being interrogated by the police. There's a picture of her and everything,' Tómas said, clearly displeased.

'The couple who run the ski lodge,' Ari Thór said. 'It must have been them…'

'There are no secrets in a little town like this,' Tómas said, his face slightly flushed.

'So what's Ottó's interest in this case?' Ari Thór asked.

'That's what I'm wondering,' Tómas said, grimacing as if he knew something he wasn't prepared to share just yet.

Ari Thór waited patiently.

Tómas sighed. 'Well, to start with, I'm led to understand that

Gunnar's job as mayor is under Ottó's patronage, that Ottó selected him and pushed for him to be appointed, even when there were other applicants who were no worse, and possibly far more experienced. He got his way, which must have been a bit of a struggle, because Gunnar is an outsider who had never set foot here before. There were two other candidates, from different parts of the town, so you can imagine that there was some rivalry that would split the vote. That definitely gave Gunnar an advantage. And Gunnar brought Elín with him. One thing leads to another.'

'You said "to start with".'

'You're sharp this morning, aren't you?' Tómas said, a smile fleeting across his lips. 'I was chatting to the teacher – Ingólfur – and his wife last night. They're devastated, completely distraught that his shotgun might have been – and almost certainly was – used in the assault.'

'I can well believe it.'

'It turns out that it wasn't just the hunting club members that knew about the gun. His wife is a member of a club as well, a group of women who fish for salmon. She said that they had all been in the garage at least once and some of them had suggested the idea of going shooting when Ingólfur's gun was mentioned. Their son also admitted that he held a party one weekend, when his parents were away, for all the kids who are graduating from the local college with him next spring. They had stored the booze in the garage … *And* they had some people over for dinner, and hunting was mentioned. The guests got up to take a look at his shotgun, and guess who was among them?'

'Ottó?'

'Got it in one. It didn't ring any bells yesterday, as then there was no obvious connection with Ottó. But he's certainly checked himself in as part of the investigation by paying you a visit.'

'So what do we do now?'

'Well, not a lot for the moment. He's not going anywhere, and it's stretching the point to call him in for an interview on the basis that he had one dinner at Ingólfur's house. But we'll keep an eye on him …'

Ari Thór looked out of the window. The dark clouds he had seen on his way to work had opened up and a combination of freezing rain and sleet now pounded the small town, puddles forming and freezing on the pavements, and the station windows misting up. Not a day to be outside, he thought, making himself more comfortable in his chair. He couldn't get Ottó's visit out of his mind, and he felt as though a line had been crossed, his home life invaded. A stranger, in this case Ottó, had come so close to his family on a peaceful night. *What if it had been the killer …* Ari Thór thought to himself, feeling the horror trickle through his body.

The nurse came and talked to me after lunch. I'd managed to get there somehow, sat for half an hour and tried to eat something.

She said she had talked to Helgi, and he said I needed to persevere a little longer and then he'd have a meeting with me later in the week. I asked if I couldn't just stop the medication.

Absolutely not, she said. We don't let ourselves be put off by a little discomfort. There are always a few side-effects with these drugs, she said. She did not meet my eyes.

21

Gunnar thought he'd arrived at work early, but Elín was there before him. They were alone at the municipal offices, but he still asked her to meet him in private in his office. She shut the door firmly behind her.

'You mustn't take it personally,' he said gently. 'That news story, I mean.'

He had been more than a little surprised to see that Elín had hit the headlines of most of the news websites that he'd looked at over breakfast.

She hesitated, trying to shrug it off.

'It's no problem. It'll blow over. There's something else I wanted to discuss … I'm very sorry about yesterday…' she said, unusually self-conscious. Normally she was decisive and focused, which was what Gunnar liked so much about her, and also found so attractive.

'Listen, don't worry about it. We were both to blame,' he said and immediately regretted using the word *blame*.

'If you want me to leave, resign…'

'Resign? Have you lost your mind? I can't manage this job without you,' he said, smiling to lighten the atmosphere.

'Of course it was completely inappropriate,' she said in a low voice, her eyes averted.

'No, it wasn't. It would have been inappropriate if I'd come on to you, as your boss,' he said and decided to come clean, feeling the blood surge through his veins. 'It's not as if it's something that hadn't crossed my mind as well, Elín…'

She visibly brightened and returned his smile. 'I thought so. It must be tough, being so far from everyone. And you have to believe that I've no intention of breaking up your family.'

'The marriage isn't everything it should be, Elín. Not any more. I have to admit it. I'm not even sure that I *want* to keep it afloat.'

She sat opposite him in silence. The next move was hers.

He heard doors opening and closing somewhere in the building as someone turned up for work.

'This probably isn't the best time to be talking about this. Shall we get a coffee after work, maybe?'

'That would be perfect,' she said, decisive and collected, and now he recognised the Elín he knew so well; he also knew that their cup of coffee would end with them in bed together. It was obvious that their thoughts were heading in the same direction. The question was, where would be the best place to meet?

She obviously read his thoughts, because she said, 'Won't you drop by my place? I can do a decent espresso, though I say so myself.'

'Sounds good,' he said, feeling his face flush.

Elín stood up and left the mayor's office without another word.

This was certainly an unexpected turn of events, Gunnar thought to himself, but probably inevitable. The attraction had always been there, and now that they also shared a secret, his secret, the bond between them felt stronger than ever.

22

A shadow settled over Iceland's most northerly town towards the middle of the day. For once, it wasn't the shadow of the surrounding mountains, but something much, much darker.

Herjólfur had died that morning, without regaining consciousness. There were many unanswered questions, and now there would never be a first-hand account to find out what really happened on that frozen, windswept night. Had he seen his attacker? What thoughts had gone through his mind when he heard the shot and felt the impact of its blast in the cold darkness?

When he heard the news, Ari Thór's thoughts went immediately to the boy, Herjólfur's son, the young man who had been made fatherless far too young. Herjólfur also had a daughter, but Ari Thór had never met her. His sympathies lay with the son, whose situation he had been in; a boy without a father. .

What must young Herjólfur be thinking now, and how did he feel? Ari Thór had only met him once, but could see him clearly in his mind. He had appeared tough, but it was one thing to receive news that his father had been shot and to keep his composure for a short time, another to be told that it was all over.

Now Helena was a widow, this respectable housewife who had already started preparing for a funeral. She had been distant when they had spoken to her and he suspected, or feared, that the news would drive her deeper into herself and she would surround herself with a thick, defensive barrier. Could this tip her over the edge, straight back into the depths of depression?

He felt an almost tearful surge of sympathy for the family.

It brought everything back, and with a stark clarity that left him feeling more emotional than he had in years. He was honest enough to admit that he still felt deeply sorry for himself, and couldn't help but wonder if his overwhelming sympathy was in itself a form of selfishness.

Unbidden, his thoughts travelled to the question of the inspector's position. When would this be advertised, and what he would have to do to ensure that this time it would go his way? He hated himself for these thoughts.

It has been an ordinary day so far. I can see through the window that it is cloudy, trying to rain. I haven't been outside yet, although I understand that I'm allowed to now, like everyone else, as long as I'm accompanied by one of the staff. But I'm in no hurry.

This afternoon I heard that Dr Helgi had turned up, the doctor was finally in the house. You could be forgiven for thinking that doctors would be regular visitors to hospitals, but that doesn't appear to be the case, at least not here on the psychiatric ward. My daily care is in the hands of people who show little interest in me.

Wasn't one suicide attempt enough?

I'm far from being the only one who gets little attention. Sometimes the whole shift sits in the coffee room playing cards, and of course none of us inmates are asked to join in. This is what throws into sharp relief the difference between us in status. Them and us.

Hey, well … Helgi had turned up.

There was a queue of inmates to see him. Not everyone, of course, just those who had a reason to see him. Like me.

But my name was never called.

I waited, pacing back and forth. I held back as long as I could.

All of a sudden, the man had left. No more appointments on his list for the day. I lost it. The nurse had promised to book an appointment for me and she knew just how bad the medication was making me feel.

Fortunately my temporary loss of control passed quickly. Two of the staff, each of them as strong as an ox, overpowered me before I could do any damage or cause anyone harm. I certainly wasn't lacking the will. I know that all too well, and that's something that has kept me awake throughout many a long night. I've been sitting here and thinking, and doing a little writing. Things are becoming clear.

23

Elín sensed an unusual chill in the house when she returned home, a hint of a draught whispering through it. Had she forgotten to close a window that morning? Or was it just the events of the past twenty-four hours that had left her shivering? It had been a long, hard day. Elín was no more accustomed to dealing with the media circus than most people, and it had been distressing – a miserable experience – being discussed by strangers all over the town and the country, without any way to influence whatever they might be saying. She had even been foolish enough to take a look at the tailback of comments that trailed below the news item on one website. Of course she shouldn't have done it, but once she had started reading, she was unable to tear her eyes away, compelled to know what people were saying about her; delving into crushing and vicious gossip from people she had never set eyes on, but who still seemed to have strong opinions about her and her ability to do her job. The story itself was simple enough, that she had been questioned by the police. But it was amazing how cruel some of the comments were, presumably because she held a semi-political position. Online debate had become increasingly vicious in the wake of the financial crash, as if anything could be said about anyone, especially politicians.

The only consolation, if it could be called that, was that the news of Herjólfur's death had come the same day. To an extent it had overshadowed the media's facile speculation about whether or not municipal officials might have some connection with the shooting. She had to admit that if Herjólfur had to go, then he couldn't have chosen a better day for it. Herjólfur's fate was naturally far worse than the gossip about her. She wanted to share the family's pain, trying her best to conjure up some sympathy, but it wasn't easy. She had hardly known Herjólfur. She had enough problems of her own.

Then there was the picture, that damned photo next to the news article. She had tried to get away with using a new assumed name, but her real name, Elín Einarsdóttir, was no longer a secret in Siglufjördur, and the journalist behind the first story that morning had clearly done his homework. The news item was about Elín Reyndal, Siglufjördur's deputy mayor, and it included a photograph of her with her real name in the caption beneath it. It was an old picture, but that wasn't the point. Now that her cover was blown, it was only a matter of time before Valberg would track her down and realise that the woman who had left him, who had fled his abuse, had hidden herself away up north in Siglufjördur.

The question was how far he would go? Would he bother to get in touch? She was sure that time was on her side, and maybe Valberg had found another woman. *Some other woman to mistreat?* Maybe, but Elín didn't care about that now. She needed to think about herself. She had to summon all her courage and stop playing hide-and-seek, look that bastard in the eye. *Far easier said than done.* She wasn't sure she knew him well enough to be sure just how far he would go. *If you leave, I'll kill you!* Had that been an empty threat? It was impossible to tell, but deep inside she knew that he was a dangerous man. That was the reason she had done all this, taken another name and let herself vanish.

Elín put down her handbag and switched on the coffee machine in the kitchen. She took off her overcoat. She would have preferred to wear a padded down anorak to insulate herself from the winter chill, but felt that wasn't right for someone in her position. So she shivered in her overcoat instead. This damned wind, so bitingly cold, virtually every single day. The mountains provided some shelter, but when the wind was from the north, straight from the sea, there was no respite from it. Today had been cold, but finally there was a long-awaited break from the relentless rain.

Goosebumps raised on her arms and the back of her neck. There was no mistake, the flat was unusually cold. A window must be open, maybe upstairs in the bedroom. She knew she ought to run up the stairs, but hesitated, suddenly afraid, alone in this echoing house. Accustomed to smaller flats in Reykjavík, she had never had so many square metres of property all to herself. But now she found that the advantages of having a large house might not be as positive as they seemed.

She tried to shake off the disquiet, reassured by the familiar hiss of the coffee maker. She couldn't put it off for long. She would have to go up the stairs to shut the window. Quite apart from that, eventually she'd have to go upstairs to bed. But that could wait, coffee first, and then she hoped that Gunnar would turn up. He could hardly have misunderstood her invitation. If he was ever going to give up on his dysfunctional long-distance relationship, now was the time; he was being given the chance to take the first steps tonight. *He would come.*

Elín stood motionless and watched the drops as they filled the little espresso cup, a shot of energy after a long day. Every time she had bumped into someone at work, she hadn't been able to help but wonder, *Has he read that story about me? Does he think I shot a cop?* Gunnar had offered her the chance to go home early, take a day off sick, but that would have meant giving up too easily. That would never do. *Let them think what they like … it'll blow over…* She hoped it would. She was in a political job, to some extent at least, and would have to get used to both the ups and downs and the attention, positive and negative.

Maybe it was for the best, a chance to step out of the shadows and forget that loser, Valberg? She would have to screw up her courage to stare him down if their paths were to cross again.

The first sip was perfect, a shot of caffeine that gave her renewed energy. The heat of the coffee warmed her through. She went into the larger of the two lounges and looked out at the snow-decked mountain slopes that rolled gently down to her back garden. Gunnar lived not far away, in the shadow of the same mountain.

'My love.'

Two innocent words shook her to the core. Wonderful words under the right circumstances, but not here, not now. Elín stood rooted to the spot, unable to move, forgetting to breathe; a chill rippled through her like an electric current.

'My love,' he repeated. She dropped the coffee cup and saw it shatter into fragments, the coffee staining the white tiles a rich brown. She sensed that she was close to losing consciousness. She would have to sit down, but that would mean turning round.

It would be best to do it right away, meet his gaze. Of two impossible options, the worst one was to have her back to him. She took her decision and spun round.

He stood at the bottom of the stairs, dressed almost exactly as he had been when they had met for the first time in that nightclub in Kópavogur. He always dressed in a similar way; jeans and a leather jacket, both of them a size too small for him. The T-shirt under the jacket was the only variation in his daily wardrobe.

Steady steps took him towards her. Should she scream? Attack him? Run? Try to get out? She decided there was nothing to be done; she had to trust her instincts. Somehow she felt it was best to keep on the right side of him, do nothing to anger him.

'What are you doing here, Valberg?' she said, hoping to sound confident, the one in charge, but her voice failed her. The words came out uncertainly, quivering fearfully.

'What are *you* doing here?' he asked, raising his voice. He was now close to her, close enough to touch her if he were to reach out a hand, or if she were to try and call for help or run for it.

She knew then that he was not prepared to let her out of the house, that he wasn't going to leave quietly. *Could she talk him round?*

'I … I was offered a job,' she said and there was a pause. 'How did you find me?' Her voice was regaining its strength. But she was still shaking with fright, scared to the point that she could barely focus.

'How did I find you?' Valberg laughed. 'Why? Were you in hiding?'

'No. Nothing like that.'

'I saw a picture of you this morning on some web page. So here I am. Got in the car and came straight here. Elín Reyndal!' he added with a laugh. 'So what's this bullshit? Did you really think I'd never find you? You thought you could hide away in this fucking dump forever?'

He stood silent, his rapid breathing a testament to a long tobacco habit.

'You know what, Elín…?' His voice dropped. 'You know what? I reckon we could have parted as friends if only you had talked to me. I know I could be heavy-handed sometimes, but I was always sorry. And you can't just do that to me, vanish like that. One, two, three, gone! Eh? People just don't do that kind of thing!'

He stepped closer, laid a hand gently on her shoulder and then raised it to slap her.

The stinging pain shocked her, and Elín instinctively tried to push him away. He grabbed both of her arms and gripped them tight, his eyes boring into hers.

This was just the start. This was going to end badly.

'How did I find you?' Valberg smirked again. 'I've missed you so much, sweet Elín! I searched for you everywhere, asked everyone about you. The national register says you live at your mother's place. Well, I've been keeping an eye on her house and never saw you. Then you get caught up in some murder case? Well, that was a stroke of luck! You shot the cop, did you?'

Valberg was flushed and trembling with suppressed nervous energy. That fire within him had been stoked and she knew that whatever he might have felt when she first left him had grown into a burning rage that had now enveloped him.

She said nothing. He held both of her wrists bunched together in one of his heavy hands.

'Anyway, that doesn't matter, my darling. It didn't take long to find you. I just asked a few people. Everyone's so helpful out here in the country. Everyone trusts everyone else! Nice house. It'd be pretty fucking good to live here, eh? More space than the block in Kópavogur! And I see you're careful about security. There wasn't an easy way in. Windows locked, doors locked. So I had to climb up on to the balcony and go in through the French doors. Only had to break one window. I didn't want to alarm you right away, my love. Because then you might not have come in … And we have stuff to talk about, so we can make sure this doesn't happen again.'

'Shall … Shall we sit down?' she suggested.

He slapped her again, harder this time. The pain stung and brought tears to her eyes.

'Go on, cry. I don't care,' Valberg said. 'It's your own fault. You can't imagine how angry I was, my love. Angry and frightened. People just don't do that kind of thing,' he repeated.

She didn't dare say anything, but felt the tears flow down her cheeks.

'You haven't even dyed your hair or cut it differently,' he said, running a hand through it. 'What kind of escape strategy is that? New name, new place, but the same old Elín. You have to do things properly, that's what I always say. You weren't careful enough.'

She thought of Gunnar.

Was he the only one who would be able to save her? She caught herself in silent prayer, praying that Gunnar would come soon. They'd set no definite time, just an almost unspoken agreement that he would follow her home.

Hopefully … hopefully he was on the way. She would scream out to him the second the doorbell rang, run and try to open the door, which was still locked. Valberg would hardly take them both on, more likely he'd steal away and…

The thought of Gunnar gave her a taste of hope, but she knew it was hopeless. If she knew him at all, Valberg would never give up. He would try again, and again, until he got what he wanted. And she was now looking at the end. Her end.

At the morning meeting I was pressured to take part in occupational therapy, so I signed up for carpentry. The other option was needlework, which isn't my strongest suit. I can do some woodwork, but I don't like it. It's two hours a day and they pass terribly slowly. We can have the radio on if we want to, but that makes things even worse with dreary classical music that might be fine under other circumstances. Here, it does nothing but add to the gloom that this community can do without. Sometimes the newspaper headlines are read out, which isn't much better. Every now and again there's some lighter music, something with a beat that lifts the mood a little.

What happened the other day has been forgotten, or so it seems. I doubt that I'm the first inmate on the psychiatric ward to lose his temper, and I don't suppose I'll be the last. All the same, I'm ashamed of my behaviour. I had in some way wanted to prove that I'm not ill. But the 'healthy' individual who 'chose' to spend a little time among the sick no longer stands out from the crowd.

I managed to get to speak to the nurse this morning. She was afraid of me. I asked her straight out why the hell Dr Helgi hadn't wanted to see me.

He is busy, she said.

Or perhaps I forgot to ask him, she said.

Forgot! I don't believe her. In fact, I could see she was lying. Either he had no intention of seeing me, or she deliberately didn't request an appointment for me.

I walked away.

I'm still taking this medication. There's no chance of getting away with avoiding it, but I don't feel well. Not well at all.

24

It could have been the news of Herjólfur's death earlier in the day that prompted Gunnar to change his mind, but he found he couldn't bring himself to visit Elín with the express purpose of being unfaithful to his wife.

He was painfully aware of his own guilty conscience, and he'd certainly had every intention of climbing into Elín's bed.

He gave himself plenty of excuses to visit her, all of varying quality, and for a while his decision had been set in stone, irreversible. He deserved it, he told himself. He had waited long enough. His wife's lack of interest had pushed him into it.

He had been excited and strained the whole day, unable to concentrate on his work. At the outset, the news of Herjólfur hadn't affected him, although he did his best to exhibit the right responses, whatever 'the right responses' were supposed to be. It wasn't as if there was a handbook to lead you through nightmare situations like these. It was obvious that people were numb with shock and the atmosphere at the municipal offices became leaden. People's eyes dropped to the floor and voices were kept low in fitting respect for the deceased, despite the all-pervading air of anxiety. The feature mentioning Elín hadn't helped. Gunnar had tried to defuse the situation with an email to the staff explaining that Elín had been helping police with enquiries and that she was in no way a suspect, but he wasn't sure it had had the intended effect.

It wasn't until Gunnar had got home, fairly early in the day, and showered and changed his clothes, that his conscience began to gnaw at him. All of the excuses that had kept his thoughts buoyed during the day, all his attempts to justify his plans, seemed trivial and weak when he heard his wife's voice on the phone. Yes, he had called her, out of the blue, ready to make his way to another woman's bed. He had sat down on the living-room floor and made the call to Norway.

His wife had answered the phone unusually quickly and she gave herself time to chat about minor things. It was as if she had somehow sensed an urgency to this call, and that their marriage was at stake. The precarious future of their relationship rested on a conversation about nothing in particular.

They talked for half an hour, an expensive half hour on international mobile phone rates, although the call was worth every penny because Gunnar stood up, took off and folded away the smart clothes that were intended to impress Elín, and lay flat on the sofa to think, sighing as he did so. He had been a hair's breadth from a move that would have been irrevocable.

He should have called Elín and apologised, even taking the time to explain honestly. But that could wait, *would have to wait*, he decided. He couldn't even think of her at the moment, let alone speak to her.

He lay on the sofa, looking out of the window, watching the darkness deepen, but feeling a new brightness inside himself.

25

'Can we sit down?' Elín finally dared to ask. 'You're going to have to let go. It hurts.'

'It's supposed to hurt!' Valberg snarled, the anger burning in his voice and his eyes. She knew from experience that he was about to lose control of his temper. She had to keep him quiet, win some more time until Gunnar would come. Valberg was capable of extreme behaviour.

'Let's sit down,' she said as firmly as she could. 'Talk things over. Let me go, I'm not going anywhere.'

He relaxed his grip. 'A good idea. If you try anything, I'll kill you. I swear that I'll kill you.'

'I'm not going to try anything,' she said, summoning inner reserves of strength to add, 'my love.'

'I know you don't mean that,' he shouted. 'Otherwise you'd never have left me.' For a moment he looked vulnerable, but Elín took care to avoid his gaze.

He let go of her wrists, but kept her within an arm's length.

She went slowly to the kitchen table. 'Shall we sit here?'

He nodded. 'Don't you try anything,' he snapped, pushing her towards a chair. She was taken by surprise. Losing her balance, she caught her shoulder hard against the corner of the table as she fell. She felt the stinging pain as she tried to pull herself up, trying not to make it obvious.

The man was dangerous, and it now seemed that his enjoyment in causing her pain was greater than it had ever been. She sat at the table with difficulty, her shoulder numb.

'I didn't come here to get you back. I know it's over between us. But no one treats me like that and I'm not letting you get away with it. Moving halfway across the country to start a new life, running away! You should be ashamed of yourself.'

'You want something to drink?' she asked cautiously. 'I think there's some beer somewhere.'

Unfortunately he was quite clearly sober. Alcohol made him drowsy, and he knew that well enough himself.

'No. No beer.'

'Can we try to fix this, Valberg? Start all over again?'

The words left a foul taste in her mouth. The man was vile. What a huge mistake she made, letting herself be fooled into moving in with him. Or, not walking out the second he first laid a hand on her…

He was silent.

'How's work?' she asked trying to sound normal.

'As if you care! But since you ask, those bastards sacked me. Fucking idiots.'

Elín's heart skipped a beat, knowing that the loss of his usual security would make him even more unstable.

Her eyes were drawn to the clock on the wall. She had invited Gunnar to drop by after work, but 'after work' could be a flexible concept. She had come home later than usual, and he had left the office before her. It was likely that he would appear soon … and her phone was in the hall where she habitually put it down when she came in. The chances that she could get that far and make a call were zero. Valberg would stop her first. Her physical fitness was good, but in a fight with Valberg there would be no question of the outcome.

'Are you serious?' he asked, his voice sharp.

'What?' She was shaken from her thoughts.

'*Are you serious?*' he repeated. 'What you said, starting all over again?'

Was he about to take the bait? Was this her escape route, for the moment, at least – not unscathed but still alive? Her cheek throbbed from the slaps he had given her and the pain in her shoulder was getting worse by the minute.

'Yes, of course,' she said, as convincingly as she could. 'Of course.'

'Prove it!' He was on his feet and grabbed at the injured shoulder. The pain was like nothing she had ever experienced. Her body could take no more and the tears burst forth.

'Go on, move!' He pushed her in front of him towards the stairs. Up!'

'Why?' she asked between sobs. 'Why upstairs?'

'The bedroom, stupid. Since you reckon there's a second chance, you must know the best way to consummate it.'

She felt she could detect the sarcasm in his voice, but wasn't entirely sure. There was only so far she could go. She wasn't getting into bed with this man for what would be nothing but rape.

'Wait,' she said.

'Wait? No! Move! Get up there!'

They were halfway up the stairs.

'Not now, my love. Not now.'

He took no notice and shoved her ahead of him.

'Not now,' she repeated, and he stopped suddenly.

'Not now? I knew you weren't serious. I fucking knew it! You lying bitch, you're nothing but a liar.'

He wrenched her shoulder from behind, pulling her off balance. At the same time, she lost her grip on the handrail. He stepped back and let her fall, watching her tumble down the stairs. Elín could feel the hammering of her heart, hardly believing that this was happening, trying to think clearly in the fleeting moments left to her between life and death. They had nearly reached the top of the staircase, and it was a long drop. She screamed in panic, hoping that the fall would not be fatal.

There are circles in the bathroom. It's strange, almost hallucinogenic wallpaper, circles upon circles upon circles … But you can get used to this just like anything else. Just like the tasteless crap they call food. Just like being ignored.

My body has mutinied against this medication but I'm not giving up. I've repeatedly asked to see a doctor, but I've had no response. I have to be careful not to let my temper run away with me, to remain calm and courteous. The nurse has promised to talk to him, but nothing ever happens.

I try not to mix with the others here on the ward. That may sound like arrogance. Some people would call it anti-social behaviour, but I don't see it like that. I've no intention of becoming part of the group in any way. I need to stay here while I recover, while I try to regain direction, so my father can forgive me. It's hard to believe, but it's true that you can invent a whole world for yourself here by not talking to anyone unless it's absolutely necessary. There aren't many of us who are inclined just to chat. People have problems of their own. The few of them, two or three people, who have a strong need to express themselves have long since found each other and they sit in the common room the whole day long, in their corner. I avoid them. And they avoid me.

26

Ari Thór went home for dinner, allowing himself a few hours to relax before returning to the station at nine. Tómas was due to chair a briefing of all the officers in the north coast region involved in the case, with key members of the team in Reykjavík listening in via telephone link. A police officer's killer had to be caught and it was clear from the ongoing attention that the case was receiving that the public expected nothing less. Things like this weren't supposed to happen in Iceland, the most peaceful place on earth. The angriest were the policemen themselves, both those in senior positions as well as the rank and file. Even Tómas had been affected. The justifiable fury of the force had its roots in some kind of natural instinct for self-preservation. 'It could have been me' and 'I could be next' were the palpable but unspoken thoughts. Although nobody voiced them, Ari Thór had no doubt that this was what was beneath the rage, consciously or otherwise.

Tómas had let him return home on the condition that calls to the station were forwarded to Ari Thór's mobile, providing Tómas with some peace to concentrate on preparing the briefing. Few of the calls received had been urgent; most were journalists, the same ones calling repeatedly and often. Nobody wanted to miss out on the chance of a scoop. In between there were the odd calls from people who claimed to have some special information about the case. Some even believed they had the solution to the crime, always something far-fetched. Finally there was a call from someone who claimed to have a message from Herjólfur from the other side. Ari Thór conscientiously recorded the details of every call, even though no reliable information had been received. There had been nothing that could warrant further investigation.

It was also very noticeable that the people of Siglufjördur had taken the killing personally. Ari Thór understood their feelings well. It wasn't just that the vision of living in the safest place in the world had turned out to be a mirage, but Siglufjördur had become the iconic centrepoint of a new and invisible menace. Previously a peaceful little town, Siglufjördur had become a dangerous den of crime. The town had lost its innocence.

Ari Thór and Kristín ate in near-silence. Stefnir was already asleep when Ari Thór came in, and Kristín appeared exhausted by a day with their son.

They watched the evening news together. The main item was naturally the case, which had been upgraded to a murder investigation following Herjólfur's death, and his career was detailed at length under a photograph that had been taken too long ago.

'Stefnir was lively today,' Kristín said suddenly. 'How was your day?'

The lack of interest in her voice made the question empty.

'It's heavy going. Tómas is more demanding than he was in the old days, which isn't a bad thing. But it's exhausting.'

'You should get to bed early,' Kristín said, her voice expressionless.

'I hope I get a chance,' Ari Thór said with a sigh. 'I have to go back for a briefing.'

'Go back? Don't you get a break between shifts?' she demanded, her irritation evident.

'Yes, but…'

The ringing of his mobile gave him a chance to leave his sentence unfinished.

There was a journalist on the line, introducing himself so hurriedly that Ari Thór didn't catch his name.

'We're putting the paper to bed,' he said. 'Any news? Anything new for us?'

Ari Thór groaned, took a deep breath and decided to let the man wait for a moment.

'No. No developments,' he said at last.

'Callmeifthere'sanything, right?'

The journalist spoke so fast that his words could hardly be deciphered.

'We'll let you know when there's anything new,' Ari Thór said, putting the phone down and turning to Kristín. 'I'm sorry, sweetheart.'

'I'm going to crawl into bed,' she said wearily.

'Already? Really? Hold on, don't…'

The phone was ringing again.

'Yes?' Ari Thór said gruffly. As he fumbled for the phone, he tried to whisper to Kristín, 'Don't go yet…'

'Is that … the police? In Siglufjördur?' It was a woman's voice, quiet, speaking cautiously.

'Yes,' Ari Thór said, frantically trying to catch Kristín's eye.

'Er … My name's … Ása.'

'Who? Ása?' he asked. He scrawled the name down. This call would have to be logged as usual.

'I wasn't sure … or…' Her voice was faint and quiet.

'Yes?' said Ari Thór tetchily. He could see that Kristín's patience was at its limit.

'You see … I wanted to speak to you about a patient on the psychiatric ward, but I wasn't sure if I should call, not really sure…'

Ari Thór rolled his eyes.

'The psychiatric ward, you say? Is that where you are?'

'What? No, no, or actually, yes. I'm a nurse.'

'And about this patient?'

'Yes…' she said and lapsed into silence. 'Listen. I'll call later, maybe. I'm sure I shouldn't be talking about patients … this was a mistake.'

'OK,' Ari Thór said, half relieved that the call was over. 'Thank you.' He hung up.

Kristín was on her feet.

'Wait, my sweet. Shouldn't we, you know, take the opportunity? Since he's asleep and I'm here…'

'Not now, Ari Thór. I'm not in the mood. I'm too tired.' Kristín moved towards the door without a backward glance, but as she reached the hall he could see her face in profile. He stood still and watched her disappear up the stairs, certain he could see tears in her eyes. Why would she be crying? What on earth was going on, and what was so serious that it could move her to tears?

I haven't left my bed this morning. I missed breakfast because I felt so ill. I'm nauseous and I don't want to be around other people. I have asked yet again for my medication to be changed, but nothing happens. I need to speak to my doctor, or just any doctor, to put in a request. But that's easier said than done. I hear he looked in yesterday, but the nurse said she didn't get a chance to mention my case to him. For a moment I had the feeling that she wasn't telling me the truth, that she hadn't asked him for an appointment.

What does she have against me?

Ása. I don't know why I never bothered to ask her name before, but she's called Ása.

There's a lonely sort of garden that I can see out of the common room window. There's nobody about, the grass is stringy and hasn't been cared for, even though it's high summer. The sky is grey, as if autumn is on the way earlier than usual. I try to peer into the windows of the building on the far side of the garden. There are far too many windows to count. Behind each one is an inmate with a tale of woe, probably sitting there by his or her window looking out over the neglected garden, just as I'm doing.

Fresh air isn't something you can expect around here. I can open my window a crack, but it doesn't do any good. I can feel the air in here getting thicker, dragging me down and my eyelids are getting heavy. Sometimes I feel that my secrets, that thin vein of evil in me, are being nurtured, growing, in this hot, sequestered place. Like a hothouse flower.

I think I'll lie down again.

27

As she came to, Elín felt her wrist break, first the sound, a gut-wrenching snap, and then the pain that washed over her in waves – a tearing, screaming pain. Nausea enveloped her and she struggled not to vomit. *Stay calm. Breathe.* She had to keep her head, if that was even possible.

But she was still alive. She had survived the fall. She heard Valberg continuing his abusive tirade, and looked up to see him at the top of the stairs. Fury had screwed his face into an almost maniacal grin – insane, irrational.

It was fortunate that it was her right wrist that was broken, the same side as the injured shoulder, leaving her left arm and hand mobile.

She struggled to get to her feet. Every inch of her body ached from the fall, and she hoped that it was only her wrist that was broken. Bearing her weight on her good hand, she tried again and this time managed to stand up. Only just conscious, she had to hold the rail to stop herself falling again, from fainting. She fought to keep her balance, her eyes fixed on Valberg at the top of the stairs. She realised that she should have tried to escape the house the moment she had seen him, run out into the street, screaming and shouting, smashing the windows, anything that would have attracted the neighbours' attention. It was probably too late now. She felt incapable of moving, let alone running, or making enough noise to raise the alarm. *Trapped.*

'You're bloody useless,' he sneered suddenly. 'There I was helping you up the stairs, and what do you do? Fall down. Lies, lies and more lies. You weren't ever going to keep your word, were you? You've lied to me the whole time, from the moment we met. I can see that now.'

She could hardly gasp out a single word. It was enough of an effort to breathe and stay on her feet.

Valberg didn't move.

'Get out, you bastard. Get out of here. I never want to see you again,' her voice was strangled, barely audible; she knew she was taking a risk, but was past caring about the consequences.

'Go? Now?' He moved down one step. 'Are you nuts? This is just the beginning.'

Elín realised that that next few seconds would decide whether she lived or died. If she stayed where she was, there was little chance that she would escape with her life. She gingerly, tentatively shifted her weight from one foot to the other. *Yes.* In spite of her injuries, she might be able to walk, maybe even to run.

He inched down the stairs, stopping halfway and watching her as a cat eyes a mouse. How far could she get? She weighed up the options. There was no way she'd make it out. The living room? Yes. The kitchen? Probably. Of course, the kitchen. She remembered the long Japanese knife next to the chopping block, one of an expensive set bought on a whim a long time ago when she had liked the idea of preparing her own sushi. She had never got round to learning how to serve sushi, but she had used the knife to slice an apple that morning. It was only sheer laziness on her part that she hadn't put it away. She would have to do something, and there weren't many options.

She ran, pain and fear – pure terror – providing her with a sudden burst of energy. She could hear him taking the last few steps down the stairs somewhere behind her.

She reached the kitchen before he could catch up with her and didn't waste time looking behind her. She saw the knife within reach, snatched it up and spun round. Valberg was only a couple of fractions of a second behind. He stopped dead at the sight of the knife.

'Are you off your head? Put that fucking knife down. We don't want anyone to get hurt, do we?' he added, his face a mask.

His last, ridiculous words brought an unlikely smile to her face, which in turn sent darts of pain shooting through her skull. Everything hurt.

We don't want anyone to get hurt, do we?

'Fuck off out of here, you bastard!'

Valberg blanched as she threatened him with the knife. Regardless of whether or not it was genuine Japanese steel, as the salesman had suggested, it was sharp as a razor and had sliced through the apple that morning as easily as if through butter. She hoped desperately that Valberg wouldn't notice that the knife was in her left hand; and hoped he wouldn't remember that she was very much right-handed. She wasn't sure she would actually be able to wield it if she needed to, but she waved it towards him, her knuckles white on the handle. She would have to focus his attention elsewhere.

'Yeah, yeah. I'm going…' he said, taking a step back. 'But I'll be back, darling. Maybe I'll move up here. Is there a place to let in the street?'

'Go to hell! I never want to see you again! Never! Understand?'

A grin crossed Valberg's face – seductive and sincere. The type of smile that always won her over in the past, but never would again.

'Maybe I'll take you up on your offer after all,' he said slowly.

'What?'

'Bed, of course. You and me, right now. Since I've come all this way. So what do you say? Or right here and now, on the kitchen floor? But you'd have to put that knife down first…' Now he took a step forward. 'Come on, give me the knife. Now!'

She felt a jolt of terror and reacted by taking a step towards Valberg, the knife pointed towards his chest. His expression changed to one of astonishment and then bewilderment, as he stepped back, catching his foot on the mat and slipping backwards as it slid out from under him. She heard the crack of his head against the kitchen table, and then there was silence.

Elín stood stiff with shock, the knife still in the air, staring at the man who had come so close to ending her life. He lay in front of her, defenceless, motionless. And she tried to make out if he was dead as she was overwhelmed by a strange feeling of calm. She edged towards him, the knife in her hand, wondering why she didn't just take the opportunity to run, or to call the police.

Was he dead? His chest was rising and falling. *He was alive.* Her heart beat faster, so rapidly that she wrestled with dizziness, everything becoming dim, as she repeated his words first to herself and then aloud. *I'll be back.* The words echoed and grew in her mind, and then in the chilly kitchen, as they beat out their unmistakable message. *I'll be back.*

Where could she hide next?

He'll be back! She had lost any capacity to think logically, and with an anguished cry, she thrust the knife away from her and covered her ears. She blacked out for a moment, and awoke to find herself sitting on the cold kitchen floor, watching the blood run in rivulets across the white tiles. She absent-mindedly thought that it took longer than she could have imagined for blood to congeal.

And then she felt herself tremble, her body wracked with uncontrollable shivers. The nausea swept over her and she vomited. Something terrible had taken place, something that could never be undone. Her body throbbed with pain, and her thoughts were a whirl of confusion. All except one, which was crystal clear. She knew, without a doubt, that she was free. Finally free.

I couldn't sleep at all last night. Those wretched drugs. Breakfast didn't agree with me either and it ended up back on the plate, much to the disgust of those present. Their reactions only made things worse and I went into a rage again. Nobody was hurt, thankfully, but it was close. I don't know what came over me. I'd like to blame the circumstances, or the medication...

Two of them sat on top of me, until I had calmed down. Now I'm under supervision. Maybe I was always under supervision. Maybe I always should be.

28

Elín waited before calling the police, giving herself a few vital moments to collect herself. She needed to think things over carefully.

There he lay, the bastard, stone dead. She felt nothing but pleasure, a warming glow that suffused her senses. The shock would undoubtedly come later, and it had to come. There was nothing everyday or normal about killing a man. But the relief she felt was so uplifting, she felt almost elated. She shook her head, as if to waken herself to the reality of the situation.

She had to face the fact she had killed Valberg. But was it murder? It would have been so much easier if his fall had finished him off. She idly picked at a loose thread on the mat – the same mat she'd nearly thrown away, just days ago, because of its tendency to slip on the polished white tiles.

She was keenly aware of the need to focus.

Whatever she had done, she felt no guilt. She could live now. Live in peace. He would never have given up without achieving what he set out to do. Sure, he might have gone to prison for a while for breaking into her home, and for the violence, but it wouldn't be a heavy sentence and she would have spent the rest of her life on the run from him. *No life.*

There was justification for this. He could just as easily have been killed by the blow to his head as it hit the tiles. Secondly, she had acted in self-defence – perhaps not in the strictest sense of the word, but it was self-preservation, and that was just as valid.

She hadn't been herself when she stabbed him, that much was clear. She couldn't remember the act itself, and Elín clung tightly to the thought that this might be her salvation. This could be her private justification, her licence to sleep at night and live a normal life as a person and not as a killer.

While these thoughts tumbled over each other in her mind, she fetched her mobile phone. She punched in the number but didn't make the call, not right away. What was she going to say to the police?

The truth? That she had murdered the man in cold blood but didn't remember doing it? Would they believe her? Maybe they would, but after a long trial and public scrutiny. She couldn't spend time in prison. That was out of the question.

That would, of course, be an injustice. Valberg had broken in, threatened her, beaten her, shoved her down the stairs and set out to rape and then probably kill her. The tables had been turned in her favour, not his. It was actually unbelievable that she had managed to get away with her life, and that bullying monster wasn't going to drag her down to hell with him.

There could be no doubt about what had happened before the end, and she bore the marks to prove it.

She made the call.

I can trust nobody here. I was asked if I'd like to go out into the garden with the others this morning, but I didn't feel like it. How long has it been since I last went outside?

Nobody has come to visit me, and that's my penalty. Dad doesn't let that kind of behaviour go unpunished. In my household nobody tries to commit suicide. Bad form.

The days pass slowly here, possibly because I flatly refuse to take part in any social activities. I have no common ground with these people, nothing!

The inmates sit and play cards, drink coffee and smoke. Yes, exactly, smoking. There's a thick fug of tobacco smoke in the common room and the television lounge. I rarely smoke myself and neither of my parents did (both suicide and smoking are frowned upon) so I'm not used to this dreadful air. Inmates get their tobacco allowance every day and make full use of it. The end result is that I feel even worse, and things weren't great to start with.

Maybe the best way to fight it is simply to start smoking. Coffee is now my dearest friend, so it shows you can get used to almost anything. But not everything, or I wouldn't be here.

29

The front door stood open. They stepped cautiously inside, Tómas taking the lead and Ari Thór close behind.

The call had come while Ari Thór was still at home. The emergency call centre had immediately directed the call to the Siglufjördur police, which was then diverted to Ari Thór's mobile.

Elín had stated her name, panting for breath and sounding confused.

'You have to come right away! He's dead!'

'Who's dead, Elín?' Ari Thór had asked in a level voice.

'Valberg, my ex. He … he … broke in. Tried … tried … tried to kill me. You have to come, right now!'

The man lying on the kitchen floor was certainly dead and the blood that had pooled around him left no room for doubt. The sight made Ari Thór's stomach turn, not helped by the long kitchen knife buried in the man's chest. Then he saw Elín, crouched on the floor, her wrist hanging at an improbable angle.

Ari Thór glanced at Tómas, who nodded and went over to her.

'Elín,' he said cautiously. 'Elín.'

She looked up at him and tried to rise to her feet. There was something odd about how she struggled, using only one hand, one arm, while the other hung uselessly at her side. Ari Thór saw the vivid marks of a blow on her cheek.

'It hurts so much,' she pleaded, when she was at last on her feet. 'He threw me down the stairs. I need to get to hospital.'

'Can you talk to us for a few minutes first?' Ari Thór asked.

An ambulance crew had arrived and they made their way across the kitchen, taking their place next to Ari Thór.

'He hit me. Again and again,' Elín breathed. 'Then he pushed me against the table and I can hardly move my arm…' She sighed and took a deep breath. 'And then … he threw me down the stairs. I think … I think my wrist is broken. It's horribly, terribly painful.' A whimper escaped her lips.

'Any head injuries?' one of the ambulance crew asked.

'Yes, I think I lost consciousness when I hit the floor.'

'We'll have to get you out of here right away.'

But Ari Thór wasn't quite ready to let her go. He switched on his recorder.

'Elín, can you tell us briefly what happened here?' he asked, his voice gentle, urging her on.

'Of course I can! He tried to kill me!' she yelled, before dropping her voice. 'I'm sorry…'

'That's all right. Carry on if you can.'

'He was here when I came home,' Elín's breathing was short and shallow. 'He climbed up on the balcony and broke in. I tried to defend myself but he was too strong. He dragged me up the stairs … and pushed me down from the top.'

She sighed, exhausted.

'We need to be quick,' one of the ambulance crew said, but Ari Thór wasn't quite finished. 'How did he receive the knife wound?'

'I managed to get to the kitchen and grabbed the knife … he was so quick … I turned round and as he rushed towards me he was … he must have landed right on the knife,' she said between sobs. 'I didn't mean to do it … I loved him once. But I had to, had to defend myself.' There was a short silence, as she suppressed a howl. 'Don't you see?' she wailed. 'He was going to kill me.'

Why is it so gloomy in here?

Dark-grey lino, dark doors, everything's miserably colourless, except the maniacal orange in my bedroom.

The food tastes foul, and I feel like shit.

I want to get away from here, but I have no desire to go home.

I remember when I first saw Dad hit my mother. Of course it wasn't the first time he hit her, just the first time that I was present; the first time he lost his temper in front of his only son.

It was Christmas Day and I sat in a corner with a toy that I had been given as a present. I looked up when I heard the smack. It was a heavy blow. I have no idea what prompted it, as it hadn't been preceded by any argument. My mother never argued. She had undoubtedly said something that he disliked. That was normally enough.

He acted as if I wasn't there. I sat stock still, watched without under-standing what was happening. It was as if I were viewing complete strangers. There were more blows. I don't know exactly how many, but more than a person should ever put up with.

I felt each blow as if it had landed on me.

Worst was the silence, the silence that preceded each blow like the lull before a storm.

I remember the glint in Dad's eyes when he finally noticed me there, and I've never seen anything like it. I was terrified. I wouldn't go so far as to say I saw evil in his eyes, that would be too dramatic. What's the best way to describe it? Anger? No … Fury, unbridled fury. That's the word; unbridled. He had no control over himself, and that's the most shocking thing, how an otherwise gentle man, strict with me, yes, but pleasant enough, could become such a monster.

A monster. I have never used that word before to describe Dad and I'm ashamed of myself for using it now, but there's a feeling of liberation in being able to write it down on paper, with no repercussions. No one can touch me here.

30

Kristín had received an unexpected phone call that evening. The doctor who had been having an unsettling effect on her these last few weeks called her from Akureyri. There was a suitably innocent reason for the call, of course; a request to take a relief shift the following day. But it was unusual to get a call of this nature from a colleague; normally this was the province of senior staff. Daydreams were innocent enough, she rationalised, as she let herself hope that he had used this as an excuse to call her, that he had wanted to hear her voice.

Their conversation had lasted longer than was strictly necessary. Stefnir was asleep and Ari Thór on duty, as always, so it wasn't as if she had anything better do than take part in a little light flirtation over the phone. It was harmless. She found it hard to believe that they had talked for almost an hour, but the evidence was there on her phone. Fifty-seven minutes had passed by the time the call had ended.

They had talked about everything and nothing, how he enjoyed living in Akureyri, what he did outside work, in the cold and the dark. He confided that he hadn't yet started to see women after his divorce. It took time to recover, even when it had been obvious from the outset that the relationship could never last.

Those fifty-seven minutes had provided her with a more interesting conversation than she had experienced with Ari Thór for months. He gave more of himself than Ari Thór did, and – she had to admit it to herself – she was more open and positive with him than she had been with Ari Thór for some time.

Before she realised what was happening, she had agreed to have dinner with him after her shift the following evening. He had complained amiably that he had no friends in Akureyri, and was getting tired of eating alone. Agreeing to meet him for dinner after their shifts meant that she had left the next move to him. It was just a meal, she told herself. That was as far as it would go.

But she wasn't going to mention this dinner date to Ari Thór. Just in case he got the wrong idea.

She felt a fluttering of excitement. Always in control, she was quick to push to one side the minor nagging of her conscience. She recalled bitterly that Ari Thór had once had a fling with that girl in Siglufjördur, so he couldn't possibly complain if she were to share an innocent meal with a colleague, although she knew inside that wasn't the case and that his frustration at being deceived, even just the perception that he had been deceived, was enough to arouse a depth of anger that she had no wish to see.

Alcohol is rarely the trigger to violence. That in itself is disturbing. Dad occasionally has a glass of red wine with a meal, sometimes a whisky in the evening if he's not on duty. But the heaviest blows are when he's stone-cold sober. That's when the anger bursts forth with added force. Alcohol numbs and soothes. Sometimes I wish, and it's not a good thing to wish for, that he was an alcoholic. Then life would be easier and better.

I had thought of drinking, but I don't think it solves anything. I have not wanted to run away, not until I sank into the depths and ended up here in the psychiatric ward. It happened so fast and was so unexpected, and I hope I can make a recovery just as quickly.

What is most painful, if I'm entirely honest, is not being able to have a sincere, warm relationship with my own parents. Dad is so distant. It is as if a gulf has opened up between us, and it is a gulf that becomes wider every time he uses his fists. My mother shows no reaction. She becomes distant in her own way, secreted away inside her shell. She's given up, and we cannot have that.

31

When the doctor had examined Elín and set her broken wrist in plaster the two police officers were finally able to take her statement . She had been fortunate; there was no need for surgery. Although the hospital had wanted her to stay in overnight for observation, Elín had been adamant that she was fit to leave despite being aware that she ought to have done as the doctor advised.

On top of everything else, she had cracked several ribs, however, these would not require further treatment. The damage to her shoulder was not as serious as she had expected, but every part of her body ached, and she had been given some powerful painkillers to take with her. She was finding it difficult to grasp the fact that Valberg was dead, but she had an overwhelming, instinctive feeling that she was now safe.

She was deeply worried that the matter would be pursued further, that she would be prosecuted for killing a man. The police officers advised her to get a lawyer, but she wasn't going to do that, not right away. She was the victim here – that much had to be obvious – and she could see that both police officers agreed with that. They believed her, and throughout their interview she had stuck to the truth – *mainly* the truth, that is. They were courteous and calm; there were no evident attempts to set any traps, and her injuries told their own tale. That vicious man was dead and she sensed that there was a tacit agreement between her and the two police officers to leave matters there.

It had occurred to her that they might take her into custody, given the severity of the crime, but it wasn't mentioned. Ari Thór suggested that she should spend the night in hospital, which she refused outright. In spite of everything, she could look after herself, with the help of some decent painkillers. There was, however, no way she could return to her home, which was now an official crime scene. Her next best option was to call on Gunnar.

He was the man she loved, but who had let her down just when she needed him the most. Why hadn't he come that evening? Now she would take him by surprise, stay overnight and tell him the whole sorry story and see him eaten up with remorse that he hadn't been there to save her, and maybe save a man's life.

'Elín?' Gunnar said, his jaw dropping in disbelief as he took in the battered figure on the doorstep. 'What? What happened?'

He looked past her to the police squad car in the street behind her. The car drove away as he closed the door behind her.

'Valberg,' She said. 'Valberg is dead. He was waiting when I got home.'

He sat in shock as she told him what had happened, but he kept himself at a distance.

'You take the bedroom,' he offered. 'I'll sleep down here.'

Elín shook her head.

'It's all right. I can sleep here. Not that I expect I'll get to sleep easily.'

'Come on. You're hurt, and you're not going to be coming in to work for a while. Take the bedroom. I won't wake you up when I leave in the morning.'

'If you insist,' she sighed, too exhausted to argue.

She wasn't going to sleep right away. She couldn't bear the thought of lying down and closing her eyes after everything that had happened, in spite of the fact that she was completely exhausted.

Gunnar sat with her in the living room and they spoke openly, like good friends do. No more than that.

It was just a matter of time, she felt, before they would take the next step.

32

After driving Elín to Gunnar's house, Ari Thór arrived at home just before eleven to find Kristín already asleep. He was almost relieved, as the tension that had been gathering between them had become an unwelcome encumbrance, and he already had enough to worry about.

The ringing of his phone broke the silence. He didn't recognise the number, but the voice that greeted him – hoarse with decades of tobacco smoke – was both familiar and unsettling.

'Ari Thór, my friend…'

'Who's that?' he asked, although he already knew the answer.

'This is Addi.'

'What do you want?' Ari Thór demanded, not even attempting to be courteous.

'Just wondering if you'd meet me for a chat?'

'Meet you? When? What for?'

'Well, tonight would be good. I might have some information for you.'

'Tonight? Do you know what the time is? Can't you just tell me over the phone?' Ari Thór could not keep the impatience out of his voice.

'Take it easy, my boy. This is just business, you get me?'

'What?'

After a long day, Ari Thór felt the weight of fatigue dragging him down, but he was still curious. He had little trust in this man, but there was a chance that he might have something interesting to say, something that would contribute to the investigation. Addi would have to be made be aware that Ari Thór was not intimidated by him, that any meeting would be on the young police officer's terms. Ari Thór wasn't going to be scared of a man who wouldn't see sixty again.

'You're at home, are you? I'll come to your place.' Ari Thór said.

There was no way that he would invite Addi into his family home; the mere thought of it was repellent, and he made that clear.

'Fine. I'm at home, as usual. I'll be waiting for you.'

'OK.'

'And, just one thing…'

'Yes?'

'Don't bring Tómas with you.'

Alarm bells rang in Ari Thór's head. While it hadn't been his intention even to alert Tómas to this meeting, he wondered why Addi had wanted to set such a condition.

'Why not?'

'It's you I want a chat with, Ari Thór, not my cousin. Deal?'

'On my way,' Ari Thór said abruptly, ending the call.

⊕

Ari Thór was sure he could smell the stench of stale cigarette smoke before Addi had even opened the door.

'Come in,' Addi said. He wore the same tattered sweater he'd had on when they had met before and there was an air of quiet triumph about him.

Ari Thór followed him into the living room, already starting to regret his decision. The filthy old furniture made him feel that he had fallen into a time warp and been trapped in this old house where it felt that nothing had been changed or even cleaned for years as the layers of dust had built up on the old-fashioned furniture left over from a past generation.

'Sit yourself down.'

Addi sat in the same place he had when Ari Thór and Tómas last visited, in the old, wine-red armchair.

'I can't stop long,' Ari Thór said, remaining on his feet. 'What do you have to tell me?'

'Quite right. The family's waiting. Kristín and Stefnir.'

'Keep them out of this, will you?' Ari Thór snapped, his anger and discomfort getting the better of him.

'Easy, take it easy. You arrested Elín Reyndal just now, didn't you?'

'You seem to know more than most people do, Addi. I'm sure you can fill in the gaps for yourself.'

'Word gets around fast in a place like this, especially when you know someone who works at the hospital … The word is she killed a man, some bastard scum who had been beating her up. Good for her, I say. Good for her!' Addi said, and grinned broadly.

'You asked me here to swap gossip?' Ari Thór was becoming impatient, even as the hairs raised on the back of his neck.

'I didn't want to say so over the phone, but I reckon you and I can come to an arrangement.'

'An arrangement? What sort of a deal do you think I could make with you? Or *would* make?'

'I have some info and you can do me a favour in return.' Addi coughed and the broad smile reappeared. 'The main thing is that I'd like to help you find out who killed Herjólfur. People shouldn't shoot cops. This is dangerous ground for all of us…'

'So what do you know?'

'Let's talk about a deal first.'

'I'm not doing any kind of a deal.'

'Easy, easy. This just needs to be a gentlemen's agreement.' Addi reached over to Ari Thór and extended a hand. 'Get my drift?'

Ari Thór ignored the hand. 'What do you want, Addi?'

'You leave us in peace.'

'You? What does that mean?'

'It means my friends and I can carry on with our discreet little business. It's nothing major – no violence, no smuggling. Just a bit of business, while you concentrate on other things…'

'Discreet business? Just what are you saying, Addi?'

'Don't be stupid. You know well enough.'

'Are you off your head?' Ari Thór said, struggling to control his temper, furious that this man should be asking him to betray his own principles as well as break the law.

'It looks like you'll be taking over, now that Herjólfur's dead. Tómas is going back south, so this is none of his business. We need to find a way to work together, you and me. I won't get in your way, and you turn a blind eye when there's a little business going on. Keep the peace, Ari Thór . You know what I'm saying.'

Ari Thór sat in silence.

'Think it over. The offer's on the table and everybody wins. You might solve Herjólfur's killing, and my friends won't be bothered too much by the police.'

'And this information? You know who shot Herjólfur?'

'Are you going to think it over?'

Ari Thór hesitated. This was an agreement he could never accept. Siding with, protecting, a known criminal would make him one himself. He would never be able to face Kristín or his son, nor look at himself in the mirror, if he bent or broke the rules like this. He shifted uncomfortably. Would it do any harm to let it seem that he might be prepared to think it over? He had a responsibility to find out who killed Herjólfur. He owed him that, at least. Addi had also mentioned Elín. What did he know about her? How much did he know about the whole case?

'Well? You're going to think it over?' Addi repeated, drawing on another cigarette, and coughing; a layer of smoke had collected, hugging the ceiling.

Ari Thór nodded, immediately feeling a surge of disquiet at the thought of accepting such conditions, making a pact with the devil.

'That's all I'm asking,' Addi said in a relaxed tone. 'You let her go, the girl?'

'Elín?'

'Elín, yes.'

'Yes, we let her go. Does that matter?'

'No,' he drawled. 'Not really. You'll just have to go and pick her up again.'

'Why?'

'She's been buying now and again, or so I'm told.'

'Buying dope? From you?'

'Ari Thór, my friend,' Addi said, with his peculiar irritating laugh. 'I don't sell dope. I'm an old man drawing his pension. We can agree on that, can't we?'

His voice became louder and he stuck out his hand again. Ari Thór sat still and could feel a nervous sweat breaking out on his body.

'Silence is as good as a yes,' Addi mumbled, and withdrew his hand. He looked recalcitrant, nothing more than a disobedient child.

'What do you know about Elín?' Ari Thór asked, his gaze firmly on Addi.

'No names, understand?'

Ari Thór nodded.

'And this is an anonymous tip-off, all right?'

'Anonymous,' Ari Thór agreed.

'She sometimes bought prescription stuff.'

'What sort of stuff?'

'Heavy-duty painkillers. The sort you can't get from a chemist without a prescription.'

'And you think this might be connected to the assault on Herjólfur?'

'Could be, couldn't it?' Addi said cheerfully.

'Could be? Why's that?'

'It's just that she used to go sometimes to collect her gear at that place. You know, the house where Herjólfur was shot.'

I hate it here. I feel bad, both physically and mentally, and I loathe it. Writing this stuff down does nothing to make it more bearable, seeing it in black and white just emphasises how lousy I feel.

There's a television in the common room, but it's summer, so the state broadcaster has closed down for a month. Just my luck to be locked away on a psychiatric ward in July. There isn't a lot to break up the day. Sometimes there are entertainments in the evenings. To start with I stubbornly refused to attend, but today I gave in.

Evening entertainment. It's an old expression that conjures up past times. There's something comforting about the whole thing, something reliable in the monotony of it all.

Sometimes, in fact, quite often, I think of my mother.

If I had a sister, would she be like Mum? Clever and hard working, but without ever having followed her dreams, fulfilled her ambitions?

Do people start growing into their parents the moment they first draw breath, with the similarities becoming successively closer as time goes on? Or is there are tipping point somewhere? If so, when?

Dad has always worked long hours, and that has become worse in the last few years, with more responsibility and longer shifts meaning extended absences. And more. I know now that I am alone in all this.

It's surprising what you can learn on a psychiatric ward.

33

Even though it was late, Ari Thór rang Tómas as soon as he had left Addi's house, giving him a rough outline of their conversation, but without mentioning the conditions Addi had set in return for information.

He would have liked to have asked Tómas if there had been such an arrangement in place between the cousins in the past, but he knew it was a question he could never ask, just as he knew that Tómas would never answer it.

They discussed how best to respond to this new information. Was Addi a reliable source? Tómas seemed to think that he was, but they agreed that it would be difficult to keep their informant's identity secret. If nothing else, it gave them a good reason to speak to Elín again. The question was whether or not it could wait until the following day.

Tómas took the decision to strike immediately. Ari Thór didn't protest, but he felt a twinge of guilt about interrogating Elín after the terrible experience she had been through that day.

They set off to Gunnar's house. It had been a surprise to Ari Thór that Elín had wanted to go there, but she had said that she had to be with someone she knew and trusted to talk things through. She didn't seem to be concerned about what the vicious tongues of the local gossips might have to say.

'It's all a myth,' Tómas said, almost to himself, as they drove. The wind had picked up considerably and a storm had been forecast that night. It was nothing unusual – with winter approaching and the days becoming noticeably shorter, he knew that this time of year could see dramatic changes in the weather, sudden snow or a rapid thaw with driving rain. A sharp wind blew from the north. It was cold, bitterly cold, even in the solidly built patrol car. Ari Thór shivered and tightened the scarf at his neck, digging his hands deep into his pockets.

Ari Thór raised an eyebrow at his colleague, curious to discover what his mutterings meant.

'A myth,' Tómas repeated. 'We imagine that we live in a country where there are no weapons and no violence,' he said, with an unusually grim expression on his face. 'The reality is somewhat different. There are far too many firearms here. I heard the figures that were quoted on the radio, not that I needed to be told. Almost every second person I know has a firearms licence. It's a myth that this place is peaceful. No violence in Iceland? That's bullshit. Sure, it all looks quiet and friendly on the surface, but behind closed doors there's an uncomfortable secret. Domestic violence; and nobody wants to acknowledge it, let alone talk about it.'

They stopped outside Gunnar's house. Tómas switched off the engine and continued speaking. Aware that Tómas had something on his mind, Ari Thór knew it was best to stay silent and let him keep talking.

'And that useless piece of shit got what he deserved today … Yes, I know I shouldn't say that kind of thing. But I'm tired and I'm angry, Ari Thór. I won't deny it. I was bloody livid when I saw the treatment that woman had received,' Tómas said pausing for breath, his face flushed. 'Maybe the bastard was simply evil. Who knows? I can tell you, Ari Thór, that violence can be found everywhere – not just in the scum, but also in men who look thoroughly respectable. Heads of families in responsible positions, exemplary citizens in every way, except when they use their fists on woman and children. I know this. I've seen it with my own eyes, far too often.'

The dashboard clock showed it was almost one. Ari Thór was exhausted and however much he sympathised with Tómas's anger, he needed to rest and longed for sleep.

'Shouldn't we wait until the morning, Tómas? It's been a long day for her, and for all of us. I expect they're both fast asleep.'

Ottó's words of warning flashed through his mind. It probably wasn't a smart move to be pestering the mayor and his deputy in the middle of the night. But Tómas wouldn't be moved.

'We're investigating a murder, and you know as well as I do that this is no ordinary murder enquiry. Someone shot a police officer. Don't forget that, Ari Thór. If we have to interrupt someone's sleep, they'll just have to live with it. This case is a priority. Herjólfur is a priority.'

They stepped out into the biting northerly wind, strong enough to set the street lights swaying gently. The darkness was overwhelming as Ari Thór battled against the gusts. He almost looked forward to the days of white winter snow, even though at times he still felt claustrophobic when the weight of snow on the town was at its heaviest.

Tómas hammered on the door, and they didn't have to wait long before the mayor answered it, fully dressed, wide awake and frowning.

'What now?' He made no attempt to hide his impatience.

'We need to speak to Elín. Is she still here?'

'Of course she is. But can't this wait? You must surely understand that she's not in the best frame of mind to be receiving visitors right now.'

'Could we come in for a few minutes?' Tómas asked, firm but polite.

Gunnar hesitated before answering, his shoulders slumping. 'All right, a few minutes.'

Elín sat in the living room with a coffee cup cradled in her hands. She looked at them, clearly tired, her eyes blank. She said nothing.

Tómas glanced at Ari Thór. He could imagine what he was thinking. Should they speak to her here, or to take her to the police station?

'Could we have a quiet chat?' Tómas asked, looking first at Elín and then quickly at Gunnar.

Considering the circumstances, Elín replied with remarkable calm. 'We can talk here. I want Gunnar to stay.'

'It's not standard practice,' Tómas said doubtfully, his expression mirroring an internal debate. He paused and sighed. 'All right. If that's the way you want it,' he said quietly, decision made.

Ari Thór noticed that Gunnar took a seat some distance away from Elín, as if making the point that they weren't as close as some people seemed to think.

For a moment nobody said anything. Tómas made no indication that he expected to manage the situation. Ari Thór had the information, so it was up to him to lead the questioning.

Eventually he took the plunge. He felt uncomfortable there, the uninvited guest in someone's home in the middle of the night.

'I ... we have witness evidence, Elín, that you have been in contact with someone dealing drugs, in the building where Herjólfur was shot.'

It was as if a hand grenade had been rolled across the living room floor. Elín sat stiff, the amazement and fear clear on her face. Gunnar looked astonished, even horrified, uttering a loud gasp as his jaw visibly dropped. Maybe his feelings for Elín were stronger than he would like people to know?

Elín finally stammered a few words. 'I ... I thought you wanted to talk about Valli ... what happened this evening ... I, er. I don't know if I should...'

Ari Thór almost expected Gunnar to rise to his feet and take a stand, arguing, demanding that they leave. Instead he sat motionless, without a word.

Ari Thór would have preferred to be more gentle, to shield this poor woman from the painful questions that were obviously distressing her, but her reactions demonstrated that a determined approach had been the right one, perhaps even bringing them a step closer to solving the mystery. Had they even found the attacker? Could Elín have murdered Herjólfur?

'Is that right?' he persevered. 'That you did some business with a dealer out there?'

Elín appeared to be in shock, her silence almost a presence in the room. Her eyes darted around, as if she was trying to make up her mind about whether she should tell the truth.

'It's best to make a clean breast of it now,' Ari Thór said more gently. 'It doesn't look good, and lies are only going to make matters worse, Elín.'

'I'm sorry, I haven't lied…' she said. 'It wasn't dope … not dope at all. I don't do that stuff. You don't think I shot the man, do you? I had nothing to do with that,' she said, speaking rapidly, her voice shaky, terror evident on her face.

'Not dope? What, then?'

'Just painkillers. Just some fucking painkillers!' She buried her face in her hands and then looked up through the tears. 'I'm sorry, I haven't come to terms with what happened this evening. Can we talk about this tomorrow?'

'We have to get this straight now. Maybe it's best if you come with us to the station.'

'No! No, I couldn't … Not now,' she yelped, her shoulders shaking.

Ari Thór pressed on. 'How much did you buy? How often? Why?'

Elín shook her head and said nothing.

'How long have you been using prescription drugs?'

She shook her head again and mumbled. 'I'm not … I … I don't want to talk about it.'

'Was Herjólfur investigating you?'

Elín gave no reply.

'Is this something Herjólfur had discovered?' Ari Thór asked. He glanced at the mayor, who seemed to have no idea what to do, what he should say, or if he should say anything at all. Ari Thór waited for his reaction, a shout, a call or even some kind of insult. But when there was no response, he decided to change tack.

'Did you have to kill him?' he asked Elín calmly.

Elín sobbed and she looked to be on the brink of a nervous collapse. Ari Thór glanced towards Tómas, who shrugged, abnegating responsibility even though he had been determined to make the visit.

'Did you…?' Ari Thór repeated, and this time Elín interrupted.

'I didn't do anything!' she yelled. 'I didn't kill him!'

'I reckon it's best that we take this down to the station.'

'No ... I don't want to go ... I haven't done anything.'

Now Gunnar intervened, with more composure than Ari Thór had expected of him. He stood up.

'That's enough. She can't take any more of this,' he said. 'I can explain. I'll give you the truth. But that will be the end of it for now. Let her rest.'

For a moment Ari Thór thought that Gunnar was going to admit to the murder.

'All I'm asking is for some consideration, for both of us, as much as is possible. Of course neither of us murdered Herjólfur. I don't imagine that has even crossed your minds anyway, but it's best to get everything out in the open.'

He paced around the living room as he spoke.

'All the same, we haven't been entirely open with you, and the responsibility for that is mine.'

The mayor sighed and paused for a moment before continuing.

'It's true that Elín acquired painkillers by ... er ... unconventional means, a handful of times. But she did it for me.'

'For you?' Ari Thór asked in surprise.

'You see, I've had a condition that has been a problem for me.' He waved his hands, as if to lighten the severity of the situation. 'It's not serious or anything like that. But I need to have these drugs. I need to use them to function properly, especially when I'm under pressure. The first few months here in a new job were stressful. I know it's not the biggest municipality in the country, but it has still been tough, with a lot of powerful people expecting me to make a success of it. And I think I've done that ... made a success of it, I mean. So far.'

Gunnar came to a halt in the middle of the living-room floor.

'And you sent Elín to that place, to pick up your dope?'

'I wouldn't call it dope ... I'm no addict ... I'm just doing my best to get through life, in a new job, and more than likely about to lose my family ... it hasn't been easy. And I didn't send anyone

anywhere. I asked Elín if she could help me out. I was doing fine
before I moved up north, but I knew I'd be struggling if I didn't
have the right medication. Sometimes I've been able to get them
from a doctor on prescription, but normally those aren't strong
enough and I'd come to the end of the line. I couldn't keep on
asking for stronger painkillers. Listen, I didn't know which way to
turn, and it wasn't a risk I could take myself, the brand-new mayor,
a familiar face, so…'

Ari Thór looked across at Elín and saw her nod in agreement.

'That's right,' she said in a low voice. 'Gunnar asked me to help
out and I fixed it for him. As I always do.'

'And Herjólfur was investigating you?' Ari Thór asked. 'Was that
why he called you, Gunnar? Had he put two and two together?'

'What? Well, no, quite the opposite.' Gunnar paused and looked
at Elín. 'He called me to let me know that he had seen Elín up there
and that he suspected there was some dope trading going on, or even
something more than that. It hadn't occurred to him that she was
there for me.'

'And how did you two react? By killing the man who was getting
too close to the truth?'

'What? Are you crazy? Of course not. We're normal people, maybe
in an unusual situation, but normal people don't *kill* other people.'
He paused for a moment and glanced over at Elín, aware of the
irony in his word. Shrugging, he continued, 'Herjólfur must have
had his eye on more than just Elín, bigger fish, sharks … Criminals
who have plenty at stake and are used to violence. I admit I lied to
you, to save my own skin, of course. But put yourselves in my shoes.
Wouldn't you have tried to keep something like this quiet?'

At the mention of bigger fish and sharks, Ari Thór's thoughts
went to Addi.

Tómas spoke, at last.

'Could you come with us, Gunnar?'

Gunnar nodded, clearly spent. He looked over at Elín.

'You stay here, Elín. See if you can get some sleep.'

'We'll take her statement in the morning. We'll start with you now,' Tómas said.

'And then what? Will the media get hold of this? Are you going to…? I mean, will I be charged with anything?'

'The investigation will have to take its course, Gunnar,' Tómas said, his voice betraying his fatigue. 'What happens next is not my decision, but I can assure you that we don't give the media any inside information about this or any investigation. That's out of the question.'

Ari Thór had spent long enough in Siglufjördur to know that it wouldn't take long for the news to leak out. It could mean that Gunnar would be forced to resign. Maybe he'd be able to weather the storm by openly repenting and promising to deal with his problem. That sort of thing always went down well with the public. In little Iceland people were quick to forgive and quick to forget.

I went outside today. It was an unseasonably cold summer day with the sun hidden behind the clouds. There are always clouds over me these days.

I also finally got to meet the doctor. He took me off this fucking medication and he promised to look at the alternatives.

We can't keep on like this, he said. Then he said, You look terrible.

He was right, of course. I hadn't realised myself just how weak I had become. The fresh air will help, I hope.

One strange thing was that he didn't recall being asked to see me, not until today. Somehow I must have misunderstood the nurse. Didn't she promise repeatedly to ask him on my behalf for an appointment? Or say that she conveniently forgot? There is something going on, and I need to know what it is.

34

Another death in Siglufjördur dominated the morning's news, although details were sparse and no names were mentioned; a tragedy but not a mystery, as one expert put it. There was, however, one news website taking the lead on a different story, to the surprise of Ari Thór and apparently Tómas as well. It was reported that Herjólfur had been investigated for corruption a decade previously, when several police officers had been suspected of taking bribes from drug dealers. Nothing was proved and the matter was dropped, but it was something that could be relevant to the current case.

Ari Thór recalled his conversation with Addi the previous night, and felt a sudden wrench. He could see how easy – all too easy – it was to step over the line, and felt a glimmer of sympathy for Herjólfur. He wasn't going to fall into that trap. He needed to put a stop to Addi's assumptions at the first opportunity, and leave him in no doubt about where he stood. If Addi thought that he had reached a cosy agreement with the police, he had another think coming.

'It stinks, my boy. It stinks,' Tómas said, when he had read the article about Herjólfur. 'It puts us in a difficult position. We need public opinion behind us. People expect police officers to be honest guardians of law and order, everyone's friend and protector. Of course it occasionally happens that one of us puts a foot wrong, and I sincerely hope that there was nothing on Herjólfur's conscience.'

'Could…' Ari Thór began, wondering if he should continue. 'Could Herjólfur have been involved in anything similar here?'

'It had crossed my mind,' Tómas answered thoughtfully. 'I can't help but suspect that there's something behind this shooting that we may wish we'd never uncovered. Perhaps we'd rather *not* know.'

'What do you mean? Of course we need to know.'

'Do we?' Tómas asked, gazing into the distance. 'Sometimes sleeping dogs are best left to lie quietly. People have to have trust in the police force.'

Ari Thór could hardly believe his ears and wondered if Tómas was really so cynical.

'We have to finish this case, Tómas. Wherever it takes us.'

'Yes, I expect you are right, Ari Thór. I just hope that whatever the solution is, it's something we can live with.'

'Can you check out these corruption allegations?' Ari Thór asked. 'Would your people in Reykjavík know anything?'

'I expect so.'

It was almost midday. They had taken Gunnar's statement during the night and Elín's early that morning. Naturally, both of them were suspects in the Herjólfur case, although there were no direct indicators of their guilt. Both asserted that they had been asleep at home on the night of the attack, not that this provided either of them with an alibi.

Media interest was growing sharply as the town filled up with news teams. Unusually for this time of year, travel conditions were reasonable, tempting many of them northwards. There was an unusual amount of traffic in Siglufjördur, as the town was swelled by an unseasonal number of visitors from nearby towns, many keen to soak up the air of mystery.

Ari Thór had not seen Kristín since the previous day. She had left early to go to work, dropping Stefnir off with the childminder on her way. She would be on duty until well into the evening, with a long shift ahead of her. Stefnir would have to be collected before four, but the childminder could take him again that evening, if necessary.

Ari Thór had received a message from Jódís, the old lady who knew the background of the past occupants of the old house, and she asked him to pay her a visit, making it plain that she had something important to tell him. He decided that her insights were probably not an immediate priority, but he scheduled a meeting for later that day, planning to take Stefnir with him to visit her. He still hoped that somewhere among the old secrets that shrouded the place it would be possible to find the key to Herjólfur's death.

'Should we bring Addi in?' Ari Thór asked.

'Addi? Whatever for?' Tómas asked in astonishment.

Ari Thór gulped. 'Well, the news about Herjólfur ... it might be worth seeing if he had been involved in anything shady up here.'

'We don't run an investigation based on hearsay,' Tómas replied frostily.

Ari Thór knew Tómas was right, but he made another attempt, this time from a different angle that he hoped might hit the target.

'Addi gave us information about Elín, so it's obvious that he's up to his ears in this business. He didn't exactly try to hide it when we talked last night. There must be more to this.'

Tómas hesitated.

'I don't doubt it ... but will it get us anywhere? And as far as I can see, Addi has been very helpful so far. The tip-off about Elín was right on the money.'

'Let's do it anyway,' Ari Thór said doggedly. 'We can't let him think that there's some kind of special arrangement just for him.'

'Well, up to you. Give him a call and ask him to stop by.'

'I reckon it would give the right impression if we were to fetch him.'

Tómas shook his head and said nothing.

⊕

Addi sat opposite Ari Thór and Tómas at the police station, confident but clearly less than happy about being publicly hauled in. His face was a mask of fury, and he provided little other than single-word answers to the questions put to him, sometimes refusing to answer at all.

'Could Herjólfur have been involved in trading drugs in the town?' Ari Thór asked.

Addi shrugged his shoulders.

Ari Thór repeated his question with more steel in his voice. 'What do you know, Addi? Is it possible?'

Addi shrugged a second time.

'What's your involvement in the business that took place where he was shot?'

Addi sat obstinately mute.

Ari Thór's patience was starting to wear thin, his tolerance levels eroded by long days, inadequate rest, an increasingly complex investigation, and the tension at home.

'Well? Do we get an answer?'

Addi stretched in the chair, lifted his head and spoke in a voice as rasping and insolent as ever. 'I can't believe that I've been hauled down here like some criminal. I've done my time inside, thanks very much. I've done nothing and certainly had nothing to do with this attack. I may have a record, but I've never gone in for violence. You know that, Tómas, don't you?'

Tómas made no comment, but the look on his face confirmed Addi's words.

'I've even gone so far as to help you, put my head on the block by helping the filth. And what thanks do I get? Arrested! You have nothing on me, absolutely fuck all.'

'Take it easy, Addi. Nobody's arrested you,' Tómas assured him.

'I've been arrested a few times before and I know how it works, I can tell you,' Addi retorted. He seemed calmer now, the anger had cooled but it hadn't left him. 'I don't forget that kind of treatment too quickly,' he said softly, the menace evident.

Ari Thór felt a shiver travel down his spine as Addi glared at him across the interview-room table, catching his eye. Addi didn't blink as he stared into Ari Thór's eyes, making plain without having to say a word that they would meet again and next time Addi intended to come off best.

35

It was obvious that the old lady was delighted to have visitors. A laden table awaited Ari Thór and Stefnir, and he guessed that the snow-white tablecloth had been laid with the Sunday-best china. There was an impressive spread of layer cake, twisted doughnuts and pancakes, everything undoubtedly home baked.

'It's a pleasure to have an unexpected guest,' she said, catching sight of Stefnir. Ari Thór hadn't told Jódís that they would both be coming. 'I don't get many visitors. Most of my friends have gone. Now I only have a few acquaintances, like the ones you met at the church hall.'

Ari Thór stood in the living room with his son in his arms. Jódís lived in the small upstairs flat of a house that looked to date back to the seventies. He had expected her to live in one of the town's old detached houses, something that her parents might have built, or even dating back a generation further. She was Siglufjördur through and through, as Tómas had said, adding that her family had been townspeople for centuries.

'Good gracious, have a seat,' she fussed. 'I don't mean you to stand there all day long. That's what happens when I start talking.'

'We're fine,' Ari Thór reassured her, taking a seat at the table. 'It's a magnificent spread. I hope you didn't bake all this just for us.'

'I'm always baking. It's one of the things I *can* still do and I often take something sweet for morning coffee at the church. I can't read as much as I used to, and baking fills my time. Fortunately, I know all of the recipes by heart.' She winked at Stefnir.

'I don't suppose you have a high chair for the boy?' Ari Thór asked, looking around, knowing it probably wasn't worth asking.

'I'm afraid not, my friend. Afraid not. I never married and don't have any children. My late brother Jónmundur had a son, but he's long grown up and moved south to Reykjavík. He doesn't visit with his children. No little ones have been to see me for a good many years.' For a moment she looked sad, but her familiar smile soon returned to her face.

'Not to worry,' Ari Thór said. 'He can sit with me.' Stefnir was normally quiet when he was in his father's arms. Ari Thór looked intently at Jódís, reluctant to upset her in any way. 'I hope my questions the other day didn't bring back bad memories.'

'Help yourself,' she said, instead of replying.

Ari Thór poured milk into a glass from the open carton on the table and helped himself to a slice of cake.

'I'm afraid I can't help you much with poor Herjólfur,' she said, picking up a doughnut and taking a tiny bite of it. 'I don't know who shot him and I doubt that Baldur has come back from the grave to murder a policeman.'

'That doesn't sound likely to me,' Ari Thór said. The cake was good. The old lady certainly had some skill as a baker.

'How do you like Siglufjördur?' she asked. 'You've been here for a few years now, if I recall correctly.'

In a small town, a police officer was practically public property.

Ari Thór answered a few more of her enquiries, polite questions that deserved courteous replies, and it started to occur to him that she had invited him to visit her purely to have some company. He began to feel edgy and it didn't escape Jódís's notice.

'I don't doubt you're wondering why I asked you here,' she said, confirming that there was something behind the invitation after all.

'Yes…' Ari Thór said, through a mouthful of layer cake.

Jódís sat in silence and waited, maybe waiting for the right moment.

He looked around the small sitting room. It was a simple home, with little in the way of decoration and furnished sparsely. There were no priceless heirlooms and no paintings on the walls. One photograph was on display on the sideboard, a black-and-white portrait of a young man, wearing a suit, his hair combed back from his forehead.

Ari Thór broke the silence. 'Is that your brother? Jónmundur?'

There was silence again.

'That's Börkur … was Börkur.'

'One of the twins?'

'Yes.'

This came as a surprise to Ari Thór. He wondered why she had a photograph of Börkur on show.

'The one who lived longer?' he asked awkwardly.

'Yes, yes. He had a longer life,' she said. 'But he was only half a man after his brother Baldur's death and sometimes hardly even that.'

'Did he kill his brother?' Ari Thór asked without hesitating.

'No, he didn't,' Jódís said and sat silent for a long moment. 'We were in love,' she said finally.

Ari Thór was perplexed by the link, but pressed on, 'Börkur and you?'

'Yes, exactly. Börkur and me.'

'But he always lived alone?'

'He lived by himself, yes. It came to nothing between us. Everything changed after Baldur died.' There was a note of despair in her voice, regret at opportunities lost. 'I kept the photograph of Börkur and had it framed a few years ago. I can't always face the past so sometimes it stays in the cupboard. But today he's here. I went and got it out as you were going to visit. Of course it's painful to remember it all but, between us, I think it's probably for the best. And it's time the truth of the matter made its way out into the daylight after all these years,' Jódís paused. 'I think it'll be a relief of sorts to tell the story. And you're a policeman, a young man, a representative of the authorities. So this is the perfect opportunity.'

'And what is the truth?' Ari Thór asked, trying to contain his curiosity.

'The truth, my friend, is that I have a confession to make. I have to confess to being responsible for a man's death.'

Ari Thór was taken completely off guard.

'Responsibility for Baldur's death?' he asked, choosing his words with care. She had said nothing about murder, and he had no intention of using the word. There had to be something else behind this.

'Yes, my friend. That's right.'

'You pushed him off the balcony?'

'Nothing so simple,' she said, and was silent for a moment. 'You know, I'm so glad not to have to carry this burden by myself any longer. I've kept the secret for too many years. A confession is a relief, regardless of what comes afterwards.'

'What happened?'

'He tried to trick me,' she said. 'In the darkness.'

'Baldur phoned and invited me round, pretending that Börkur was there as well. He knew that Börkur and I were close. I turned up, late that evening. He was upstairs, out on the balcony. I was fooled for a while to start with, in the dark, like I said, and thought Baldur was his twin brother. It was late summer, getting on for autumn. It was warm outside, but night was drawing in. When I realised what was going on, I fought him tooth and nail. He wasn't going to let me go. Somehow I found a little bit of extra energy, not something I can explain, and I got him off me by pushing him away. And…' Her voice vanished into silence, her words swallowed up. Nothing more needed to be said.

'What about Börkur and your brother? How were they involved?' Ari Thór asked after a short spell of silence.

'Börkur and Jónmundur weren't there.'

'What? Wasn't there supposed to have been a party that night? Have I got it all wrong? I was given to understand that all three of them were present?'

'Yes, that was our story. The story we cooked up between us, that *they* cooked up. Baldur died in the fall. I was going to give myself up, go to the police, but first I wanted to find my brother. I couldn't go alone. He went and fetched Börkur, and they wouldn't have it. They refused to let Baldur ruin my life. All three of us knew that Baldur was ... well, he was nothing like Börkur. He had a dark side to him. Those brothers, the twins, they were chalk and cheese, even though they looked the same. I don't think Börkur ever mourned his brother, although he missed him. But of course, after that Börkur and I never could rekindle what we had before. The lies brought us together and tore us apart.'

She sighed, and stood up.

'Would you like me to come and make a formal statement? I'll take whatever's coming to me. It's about time.'

Ari Thór believed her account – he had no reason to doubt it. He also felt a deep sympathy for her. She'd carried the secret with her for decades, much of that time on her own, a single person living in a small flat with few friends. It didn't occur to him for a second to make her life any harder than it already had been.

'I don't see any need for that. I'll make a suitable report,' he said, although he had no intention of doing so. This story wouldn't be going any further. 'We don't pursue cases that go back that far. You don't need to be concerned about it.'

'What? Are you quite sure about that?' she asked, eyes wide in surprise.

'Quite sure,' he said with a smile, quietly pleased that he had been able to put the old lady's mind at rest, but unable to avoid comparing her situation with Elín's. Would Siglufjördur's deputy mayor find herself charged with manslaughter or even murder, even taking into account the injuries she had suffered and the long years of fear and maltreatment?

I don't know why I'm still writing, or why I haven't destroyed this book.

I'm still shaking a little, as I'm angry and scared. It's a dangerous mixture.

I decided to speak to the nurse, and find out how many times she tried to get the doctor to see me. I suffered day after day on this medication and I trusted her to help me.

I couldn't do it until today, she said.

She lied to me. More than once.

I told her what I thought.

She treated me like a child.

Did I say that? Did I promise that?

She was going to walk away, and I grabbed at her. Not hard, but firmly enough that she had to stop.

I was going to say something, repeat what I thought about her letting me down, ask her why.

Then she snapped at me: I'm twenty-seven.

It took me a moment to understand. Twenty-seven, yes.

I let her go and she ran into my room, opened the book and read out loud everything I had written about her.

'Maybe around forty. She has a slightly pudgy face; too much red wine and too many steaks over the years. Her eyes are tired and she never smiles. I can't get on with people who don't smile.'

And that was some of the better stuff.

The bitch had sneaked in and read my diary, maybe every single day.

I'm not going to let it worry me. I'm going to continue writing, but I'll take care not to leave the book anywhere and I'll sleep with it under my pillow at night.

Yes, I could have assaulted her, and I wanted to. But I didn't. I controlled myself, this time.

That has to be a sign of improvement.

36

I've never gone in for violence.

That was what he had told the police and, up to a point, it was quite true. Addi's fingers had been in many illegal pies, although his activities had always been conducted with a measure of respect for his fellow citizens.

He had been caught up in the occasional fight, but had rarely harmed anyone without provocation. But threats were part of his package and he had issued plenty of those.

An old man now, he was unlikely to change his habits, even though he was furious with that pipsqueak of a boy, Ari Thór. They had a deal, information in exchange for room to operate, and the first thing the cop did was to go back on his word and haul him off to the police station like some common villain.

The only thing on Addi's mind as he left the police station was to get his own back. He wanted to get even with Ari Thór one way or another, bring him back down to earth with a bump. There was every chance that Ari Thór would be promoted to inspector in the next few weeks and there was no question that he could be allowed to strut around exhibiting that kind of behaviour. Addi knew that he had to engineer a balance of power between them.

But he wasn't one for violence. Nobody could accuse him of that.

He went straight to Ari Thór's house, hammered on the door and waited. He meant to give the girl a fright.

There seemed to be nobody home. The thought of breaking in flashed through his mind – do some damage, just enough to balance the treachery he had suffered at the hands of the young cop. He sighed. He was far too long in the tooth to be doing that kind of thing, and there was no point in attracting too much attention to himself. There were few if any break-ins in this little town and he wanted to keep it that way. The absence of obvious crimes gave people a false sense of security, and that suited everyone.

He decided on a little jaunt to Akureyri instead. He knew a few things about Ari Thór, the important stuff, at least. For instance, that Ari Thór's wife, his girlfriend or whatever, worked at the hospital in Akureyri. Visiting her there would be just the thing. If she wasn't at home with the child, she was bound to be at work.

The drive to Akureyri only took an hour. After the storm during the night, the wind had died down to let a bright winter's day emerge.

He had to wait an uncomfortably long time at the hospital before he got anywhere at reception. It was busy, and there were not many people on duty, everything cut to the bone in these harsh times of austerity.

He asked for Kristín.

'She doesn't deal directly with patients. Have you been in touch with your GP?' asked the woman in an expressionless voice, her flat tone free of any emotion.

She looked him up and down as she spoke, as if trying to work out what might be wrong with him.

'No, you've got it wrong,' he said, as courteously as he could. 'I'm her uncle. I was supposed to meet her here after her shift.'

'Oh, I'm sorry. Let me see...' the woman apologised, placing a pair of glasses on her nose and peering at the computer screen in front of her. She showed a little more animation, as if speaking to someone with a slightly different agenda made a change from the relentless flow of patients. 'Yes, Kristín won't be off duty for another hour.'

'Oh,' he said, looking at his watch. 'I must have got the time wrong.'

'I do that all the time as well,' the woman said, and grinned at him. 'You're welcome to wait. She normally comes through this way and uses that door,' she said, pointing it out.

'All right, I'll do that. It's not worth leaving and then coming back. I live out in the east, you see.'

He had seen Kristín before and was sure he would recognise her. He had a memory for faces, always had done. It had served him well in the business. He sat and waited. He always felt uncomfortable in hospitals and this time was no exception.

After an hour sitting at reception, he spied a young woman approaching. Yes, it was her. It was, however, a surprise to see that she had a man at her side, probably a few years older. They seemed friendly. If he hadn't known better, he'd have guessed they were a couple. Could it be…? Or what?

He sneaked out ahead of Kristín and the man, before the receptionist noticed and could alert her to that fact that her 'uncle' was waiting for her.

Addi had hoped to have a chat with her in private. He didn't intend do her any harm, just give her a bit of a fright, a few vague but menacing threats. He knew from experience that that was enough to put the fear of God into most people – especially ordinary people like these, who worked from nine to five and then spent the rest of their time relaxing with their families.

Kristín and the gentleman strolled downtown. There was hardly a breath of wind to shake the few remaining leaves from the trees and the fjord was glassy calm, the lights of the town reflected in the placid water.

Addi hurried after them. He needed to talk to Kristín alone, but it didn't seem likely that the man would leave her side any time soon. They finally disappeared inside a restaurant – a pricey one, noted Addi, and quite romantic, too. Addi followed, sitting at a table not far from them. It wasn't long before he realised that maybe he didn't need to talk to Kristín after all. Maybe it would be enough to take a picture of the two of them together – to give that upstart Ari Thór a shock. A simple but effective tactic – enough to convince Ari Thór that gentlemen don't break their word.

37

When Ari Thór arrived at the police station that evening, Stefnir safely deposited at the childminder's house, he found Tómas in conversation with Ottó, the town councillor.

Ottó got to his feet when he saw Ari Thór, extending a hand as he did so.

'Good evening, Ari Thór,' he said, his voice courteous. His expression suggested something different. He was here to make clear his disappointment. 'That came out badly for us,' he said without any further explanation.

'Good to see you, Ottó,' Tómas said with finality, making it clear, beyond any doubt, that the visit was over. He turned to Ari Thór.

'Just as well you're here. We have a few things we need to go over.'

'I was just saying to Tómas here,' Ottó said. 'It seems our friend Gunnar is finished. Tómas has declined to confirm anything at all, but a man hears a few things when there are whispers around the town. If Gunnar is involved in anything to do with narcotics, then we have to be rid of him. It's a pain in the arse, a royal pain, in fact. Nothing but trouble. I've no idea who we can find to replace him and in spite of everything, we were all happy with his work.'

Ottó sighed, a disgruntled, almost petulant look on his face. 'Of course, *you* couldn't leave the man alone,' he added, more to himself than to Ari Thór and Tómas, but the message was clear all the same.

Ari Thór found these half-veiled accusations frustrating. He knew that he sometimes asked questions that were better left unasked. He also knew that this was more likely to happen when he allowed something to irritate him.

'Ottó, you know the history teacher from the college?'

'History teacher? You mean Ingólfur?'

'That's the man,' Ari Thór confirmed.

'Yes, of course. We know each other. What about him?'

'His shotgun is still not accounted for.'

'Oh, really? That was why you were at his place the other day? I heard about that, and wondered what the reason was.'

'We suspect it may have been used in the assault on Herjólfur,' Ari Thór said drily. 'The *murder*, I mean,' he added, waiting for Ottó's response.

'You don't suspect Ingólfur had anything to do with it?' Ottó asked in astonishment.

'Have you seen the shotgun?'

'How could I remember that?' he snapped.

'You had dinner at his house not long ago.'

'And what does that have to do with it?'

'You all saw the weapon, didn't you?'

'Well, yes, I suppose so, it was there, in plain sight,' Ottó said sulkily. 'I'd forgotten about that.' He was restless, clearly keen to avoid being swept into the investigation. 'If there's anything that needs to be discussed further, I'd be grateful if we could talk about it later. I'm in a hurry.'

'Fine,' Tómas said. He looked drained, black rings pressed under his eyes.

'What was he after?' Ari Thór asked, when Ottó had made his speedy exit.

'Fishing for information. He's obviously trying to decide whether to stand up for his mayor or not when the shit hits the fan. Ottó is the kind who thinks things through before jumping one way or the other, and he's certainly not going to be swayed by any sentimentality.'

Tómas paused before his voice took on a more determined note.

'Sit yourself down, my boy. Time to talk things over. Did you get anything useful out of Jódís? What did she want?'

Ari Thór had told him about the conversation with Jódís at the church hall and her subsequent invitation to visit.

'Nothing at all,' Ari Thór said, brushing an invisible speck of dust off his sleeve and avoiding Tómas's gaze. 'She's lonely and I was a suitable victim. I just let her rattle on about the old days, her brother and that sort of thing, but there was nothing relevant there. All this stuff has nothing to do with Herjólfur.'

He felt not even the slightest twinge of conscience about this lie.

'I didn't expect anything to come of it, to be honest,' Tómas said. 'But no stone unturned, as they say.'

Ari Thór nodded.

'This matter of Elín and her former boyfriend,' Tómas continued. 'This isn't our case any more. It'll go to the prosecutor, but I gather there's little likelihood that she'll be charged. It was self-defence in extreme circumstances, nothing else.'

'Not our case?' Ari Thór was taken aback. 'Don't we have to file a report?'

'I've already done that. I hope you don't mind. There's so much to do that it seemed best to get it out of the way.'

Ari Thór did mind. In fact, he was furious that Tómas was taking so much control. Strictly speaking, the Valberg case was Ari Thór's and not Tómas's. Tómas had been sent north with an assignment to assist the investigation into Herjólfur's death, and there was no indication of any link other than Elín's connection to both cases and the fact that the media coverage of the Herjólfur case had resulted in Valberg being able to track Elín down.

He decided to let the matter rest, for the moment, at least, and nodded his agreement. He could only assume that Tómas was missing his old role as the town's inspector of police. *Enough to tempt him to re-apply for the post?*

'I've also had a word with my colleagues down south,' Tómas said, and Ari Thór could not help noticing his choice of words – not 'back home', but 'down south'.

'They're convinced Herjólfur had nothing to do with any

historical corruption; they're certain that he's not ... sorry, he *wasn't* ever dishonest. Quite the opposite, he was very aware of the force's honour, and the same went for his father. Both of them were coppers to their boot-heels, honest, strict and determined. Neither one of them would allow themselves to be manoeuvred into ... involved in ... anything underhanded.'

'All the same, that kind of thing isn't easily forgotten,' Ari Thór said.

'No, no. You're right. The seeds of doubt, and all that. Now there's gossip running around that he was shot because he'd been keeping dubious company, that he brought it on himself. It's important that we protect the man's reputation, now that he can't defend himself.'

Ari Thór wasn't entirely in agreement, but he wasn't inclined to start an argument with Tómas.

'He has a family ... had a family. His wife and children ought to be the ones to defend his reputation,' Ari Thór said.

Tómas said nothing, his usual response when he didn't agree with Ari Thór.

'Speaking about family.' Tómas said. 'The boy will be coming to Siglufjördur tonight to collect a few things for his mother. I don't see any reason why that should be a problem. We've been through everything, including all of Herjólfur's papers, and there were certainly no secrets there. I said the boy could take whatever he needs to, and he could stay in the house. The widow said that she's never setting foot here again, so she sent him instead. The funeral will be in Reykjavík and they're getting things ready. And as if that's not enough, she has a broken leg.'

'Broken leg? Who?'

'Helena. Herjólfur's wife.'

'What? Did that happen recently? I saw her the other day and she was fine,' Ari Thór asked, his mind travelling back to their last visit. He recalled that she had not stood up. Not once.

'She picked up a skiing injury a while ago, or so I understand. She thought it was nothing serious and it would heal soon enough, but now it seems that the leg is badly injured ... broken.'

'All right' Ari Thór said, his mind elsewhere. He was wondering, not for the first time, how the boy was coping with the loss of his father, and whether or not he had realised quite how tough it was to lose a father at such a young age.

'I called on Elín earlier, as well,' Tómas said. 'She's on sick leave. I just hope the newspapers can treat her with a little sympathy, show some consideration. But all things considered, she seems to be doing well.'

'You believe them?' Ari Thór asked.

'What d'you mean?'

'That they know nothing about Herjólfur's death? Gunnar had plenty at stake, his reputation and his job, as we now know.'

'I'm inclined to believe that they're telling the truth … at least, I think Elín is,' Tómas said. 'I genuinely hope she's innocent … It's not only that she suffered a brutal attack by that man, Valberg, but she's going to have to live with the burden of having killed him to save her own life.'

'But let's say she *is* guilty of killing Herjólfur, for argument's sake. Wouldn't that also put Valberg's death in a new light?' Ari Thór asked.

'You mean that she set out to murder him? Come on…'

'We shouldn't rule it out.'

They were both silent for a moment.

'There's a lot of pressure on us,' Tómas said. 'We have to get this right.'

'That's nothing new,' Ari Thór said, suddenly feeling an inexplicable surge of optimism. He had the feeling that a solution was within his grasp, as long as he could work out how everything fitted together. For some reason, Valberg kept coming back to him.

I'm going home tomorrow. The new medication is much more effective, and I'm a lot better. I think. It'll be good to get away from this place but I'm nervous about it. I don't particularly want to go home. I'm sure that time has stood still while I've been away.

The doctor says I've turned the corner.

But he doesn't really know. He doesn't know why Hanna and I parted so suddenly and with so much ill feeling.

I had pretty much moved in with her, and came home one evening to her place, our place. I was tired, irritated by my parents, as always, and angry.

She said something and I don't even remember what it was. It doesn't matter now, but it was something that caused me to see red. I don't know what came over me, but I hit her. Not as hard as Dad would have done, but hard enough all the same.

She was shocked to begin with. Then I saw her feel the pain, and the anger poured out. Everything happened so fast. We haven't spoken since. I moved back to my parents' house and shut myself away for days on end. I couldn't believe what I had done. I didn't believe I had done it.

It was as if I had been infected by something malicious, an incurable sickness. There was no way to escape it. That's the way I felt and that's the way I sometimes still feel. Occasionally I hope for a brighter future, and that I can lift myself above all this somehow.

Dad came yesterday. He said it was time to come home. He had obviously spoken to my doctor or someone else in charge here because he seemed to know everything about my treatment. Then he told me I had nothing to worry about, and this spell in hospital would be wiped clean from any official documents. In other words, it would be hushed up. There would be no black mark on my file, as he put it. My career would not be affected. Of course I don't have a career yet, but we both know what he has planned for me. Maybe he wants to wipe out any record of these dark days for his own benefit as well as for the family's reputation. It's a humiliation he'd find hard to bear.

The nurse came to see me off. She was unusually warm, almost embarrassed. We both know that she had crossed the line, but I'm not going to do anything about it. Dad would never have it, anyway, as it would attract too much attention. For someone with Dad's connections and influence, it's possible to make all the records of my stay here disappear, but there will be people who will remember me, especially that nurse. And it's not as if I have a name that's all that common.

Herjólfur.

38

Kristin found Ari Thór and their son asleep when she returned home late that evening, and she didn't want to disturb them. Ari Thór had managed to get very little rest over the last few days, and he was still struggling with the after-effects of his flu.

Dinner in Akureyri had not gone well. She wondered what she had been expecting. Was it just a half-hearted attempt to be unfaithful to her husband, but without taking things too far? Pay him back for his dalliance with Ugla all those years ago? Or maybe shock him into noticing that she actually existed, and needed more from him to make the relationship sustainable? Petty revenge wasn't her style, really, and the evening had been a mistake.

Even the food had been poor and she hadn't eaten much of it. Maybe her conscience had soured her taste buds. She made herself a snack from the contents of the fridge to quash the worst of the hunger pangs. The company hadn't been everything she had hoped for, either, and there had been more excitement in the expectation of dinner with this good-looking man than in the reality of it. She had found that they actually had less in common than she had hoped, and Ari Thór had never been far from her thoughts. She had to admit that it had been a grand error of judgement on her part. Her punishment, and fortunately her only punishment, was that she would have to continue to work with this man and endure endless potentially awkward moments.

Ari Thór woke up as she crawled into bed alongside him. He turned to her, kissed her and stroked her cheek.

'Tough day?' he asked.

'Just a bit,' she said, shivering at the lie she had told, and the necessity of maintaining the fantasy that she had been on duty far into the evening. 'And you?'

'It's not been easy. I'm sure there's something crucial in this case that we've overlooked, some kind of explanation…'

He sat up in bed, and force of habit made him check his phone.

'Hmmm,' he grunted to himself. 'I need to pop downstairs to use the computer, sorry. It's a message from a guy – a local villain, in fact – about some pictures he's sent me. There's never a minute's peace.'

'All right, love,' Kristín said and closed her eyes.

⊕

She was on the verge of sleep, when Ari Thór came back upstairs. For once, he didn't try to keep his voice down, even though Stefnir was asleep in the same room.

'Can you explain this?' he demanded, a hurt surprise, fury evident in his voice. 'Can you explain *that*?' he demanded, louder this time.

He handed her the laptop. She was shaken fully awake by the photographs. There were several, not particularly clear, presumably taken with a mobile phone, but clear enough; pictures of her secret dinner date.

'When were these taken? Weren't you at work this evening?'

At that moment she knew she *could* tell a lie, but also knew that she wouldn't. She knew that she had to be completely honest and there was no way to cheat her way out of this, not if she had any intention of salvaging her relationship with Ari Thór. She definitely wanted to do her best to do just that.

'No … I was invited to dinner,' she said in a low voice.

'Dinner? Who invited you? This guy in the photo?' Ari Thór snapped.

'Yes…'

'And who is he? Who's this man?'

'Just a doctor, in Akureyri.'

'Just a doctor? Are you sleeping with him?'

'No,' she answered, hesitating unnecessarily and immediately regretting not having been more definite. *Of course not.* Something like that would have been better.

'We're just friends,' she added.

'So why did you say you had to work?' His voice was loud and it woke Stefnir, who started to cry.

She gulped again. She didn't want to lie, but the whole truth was going to be difficult.

'I … er. I thought you'd react badly.'

'Why? Because you're seeing someone else?'

Stefnir's cries became louder. Kristín got out of bed and swept him into her arms, trying unsuccessfully to comfort him.

'No, Ari Thór, we're just friends.'

Her words sounded unconvincing in the dark bedroom, even to her own ears.

'I don't believe it.' The anger in his voice seemed to have given way to wretched sadness. 'You can sleep here tonight, you and Stefnir. And you made me take him to the childminder so you could go for dinner with your boyfriend!' He was hurt, deeply upset.

'I'm sorry, Ari Thór,' she said, a sob threatening to burst from her, and realising that an apology was tantamount to an admission.

He said nothing, and disappeared downstairs, leaving Kristín with the discomfort of knowing that everything had changed. Nothing could ever be the same again.

39

Ari Thór found an interesting email awaiting him when he arrived at the police station, a message that had also been copied to Tómas. There were questions over Valberg's knife wound and the way the knife had entered his chest. It seemed unlikely that he had 'walked into the knife' and more plausible that he had received the wound where he had laid on the floor. Ari Thór was uncomfortable with the theory. He found it hard to accept that Elín was anything other than the victim, and his sympathies lay with her.

The email had been sent to him and to Tómas for their information only, making it plain that they were not expected to take any further part in the investigation.

He struggled to get to sleep on the old sofa at the station. It was too small in every direction. His feet stuck out over the end and the slightest movement threatened to topple him onto the floor. Above all, the evening's events were keeping him awake – the argument with Kristín, and the overwhelming disappointment. Of course he'd made a mistake of his own, but that was in the past, and he'd taken his punishment for it at the time.

Kristín's face, her body language, her tone of voice and of course the secrecy all pointed towards something much more than an innocent meal with a colleague. He couldn't get out of his mind how distant she had been recently. How long had this relationship been going on? It was a betrayal, a clear betrayal of him, Stefnir and their family.

What next? Should he go home after a night on the sofa as if nothing had happened?

Should he allow Addi Gunna, who had sent him the pictures, to succeed in wrecking his family? The idea was distasteful, but this was about something larger and deeper. A trust that had taken a long time to build had been swept away in the blink of an eye.

Maybe it was all over?

⊕

It was a long night. Ari Thór slept fitfully, a few moments at a time and during periods of wakefulness, his thoughts went from Kristín to Herjólfur's death and back. What had Tómas said that hadn't quite added up? And why did Ari Thór *still* feel there was a link to Valberg?

It wasn't until the early hours, as he lay somewhere between sleep and wakefulness, that the answer broke through from his subconscious. Herjólfur had told him that he and his wife weren't much interested in outdoor activities – such as skiing. But now the news from Reykjavík was that his wife had broken her leg on the slopes. Could that be a fiction? What was she hiding? The thought of Valberg kept on flashing back to him, too, as did the year's leave that Herjólfur had taken to look after his wife when she was ill. *What illness?*

Strict and decisive was how Tómas had described Herjólfur.

Tómas's tale of Addi Gunna and the rescue operation high in the valley at Skardsdalur came to mind. *Everyone has a good side to them, even Addi,* Tómas had said. *And everyone has a dark side that others don't get to see,* thought Ari Thór.

When he and Tómas had talked about Valberg, Tómas had made the point that not only criminals committed violent acts, but also men who appeared on the surface to behave impeccably, heads of households in responsible positions.

He also recalled that Helena had not seemed to be particularly upset about her husband's injuries, neither when he brought her the news, nor later when they met again. She had even started to prepare for the man's funeral before his death had been confirmed.

Could she have been hoping that he wouldn't survive?

Valberg's assault on Elín had given Ari Thór the germ of an idea … had Herjólfur possibly been violent towards his wife? Would that explain the strange, subdued atmosphere, and the lack of any apparent distress or sorrow on his family's part?

Ari Thór sat up on the sofa. There wasn't a chance of getting back to sleep.

The more Ari Thór thought about it, the more convinced he became that this possibility was something he would have to investigate.

But regardless of whether this theory was right or not, surely the assault on Herjólfur was most likely linked to the drug trading that Herjólfur had been looking into, the business that was at least partly conducted at the house where the fatal shot had been fired?

Then Ari Thór recalled how he had first found out about the investigation at the house. From a family member who had so very kindly pointed him in that direction; away from Herjólfur's personal life.

No, *hell* …

Ari Thór refused to believe it. It was unthinkable.

How had he known where the shotgun could be found?

The answer came to him in a flash. Of course this person knew about Ingólfur's shotgun. And if Herjólfur was the intended target, very few people could have known that he was on duty that night. He quickly pulled on his uniform jacket and hurried out of the police station, slamming the door behind him, out into the cold morning to meet a murderer.

I still haven't got rid of this notebook. I surprised myself by bringing it home, actually wanting to keep it. This has been an experience that I must never let myself forget, the misery and the fear, all those things that made me want to take my own life. I still find it hard to believe that I took things that far, but I still feel a shadow of the despair that propelled me towards it.

I feel as if I'm standing in front of a wall, an insurmountable wall. There is no way over it. I will never be able to escape my father's shadow. I fear that eventually I will become like him.

40

Ari Thór stood by the basement door and waited. He had already rung the doorbell twice.

The town was quiet, with night just turning into a piercingly cold morning. The darkness seemed endless at this time of year.

He rang the bell a third time. Nobody answered.

Not giving up that easily, he thought. He shivered, scowled into the frosty wind and went to the main door instead and rang the bell there. As he did so, he heard movement inside the house.

Ari Thór stood in much the same place as he had a few days previously, looking into the eyes of Herjólfur's son and namesake. Now the boy looked weary and there was bewilderment on his face. The last time they had met, the younger Herjólfur had been serious, stone-faced as he told him about his father's investigation into the old house.

'What's the matter?' the boy asked, with evident surprise.

'Could I come in?' Ari Thór asked politely.

'You know what the time is?' the younger Herjólfur asked, rubbing his eyes. 'I was fast asleep, like normal people are at this time of day.'

He stepped back and gestured for Ari Thór to step inside.

Herjólfur switched on the living room lights and nodded for Ari Thór to follow him. The living room appeared as it had before, cold and soulless. Nothing seemed to have been moved since he had been there last, everything in its place.

Herjólfur sat on the white sofa, as his mother had, the last time Ari Thór visited. He chose to stand, as he had done before. This was serious business, deadly serious if his suspicions were to be confirmed. It was as well to keep things formal.

'I understand your mother has a broken leg?'

'Yeah,' Herjólfur answered shortly. 'Yes, broken. They thought it was a sprain at first, but no. She thought it would sort itself out, but it needed to be put in plaster.'

'What happened?'

'She, well ... she hurt herself skiing.'

There was a tremor behind his voice and he did not appear to be as relaxed about this early-morning visit as he clearly wanted to be.

'Your father told me that you weren't outdoor types. He said that he and your mother never went skiing. Just holidays to town.'

The boy gulped.

'True. Dad wasn't much for that kind of thing.'

Herjólfur seemed keen not to allow this line of questioning to be pursued and Ari Thór let it go.

'I take it he made all the decisions?'

'Yeah,' Herjólfur agreed, and there was a great deal of weight in that one word.

'Decisive?'

Herjólfur nodded.

'At home as well as at work?'

'Don't know about at work.'

The answer was short, but the message was clear.

'I saw some reports about your father being linked to some corruption case down south,' Ari Thór said, watching for the response.

'I wouldn't know,' Herjólfur said. 'It's not my affair.'

Under normal circumstances a son might have been expected to leap to his father's defence in the face of such an allegation, but Herjólfur seemed to have no intention of doing so.

'Thanks for the lead,' Ari Thór said after a short silence.

'What?'

'The drug trade at the old house.'

'Yeah, of course,' Herjólfur muttered.

'You were quite right ... or your father was quite right. There were people using the place for just what he suspected.'

'OK.'

'Your mother said you live in the basement.'

'Yeah, that's right.'

'I tried the doorbell down there.'

'You can't hear it up here. I thought I'd stay upstairs. More room.'

'So you can come and go as you please.'

Herjólfur looked questioningly at Ari Thór.

'That's what your mother said.'

'Yeah…'

'Is that right? Didn't they notice if you were here or not?'

'No, I don't suppose they did…'

'And where were you the night your father was attacked?'

Herjólfur took the bait. 'Where was I?' he asked, his eyes flying open as if he was shocked by the question.

'Yes. Were you here? Asleep?'

Herjólfur jumped to his feet. 'What are you asking that for? What the hell are you asking *me* for?' For a moment the boy seemed on the verge of bursting into tears – or an angry tantrum. 'Yes, I was asleep, down in the basement.'

He sat down again.

'There weren't many people who knew about this investigation, Herjólfur. Is that where the idea came from?'

Herjólfur said nothing, and Ari Thór continued. 'The police would be looking for a dealer or a user as the killer. And the case would never be resolved.'

Still Herjólfur showed no response, although Ari Thór hoped that his questions were having some effect.

'And the shotgun, how did you know about that?'

Finally there was a response. 'What d'you mean?' Herjólfur squeaked indignantly.

'Shall I tell you what I think? I'm sure you knew it was there in Ingólfur's garage. We found out that his son was having a party for all the kids who are graduating next spring. He's in his final year, just the same as you. That fits, doesn't it?'

Herjólfur was silent.

'That's right, isn't it?' Ari Thór demanded, raising his voice a little. Herjólfur nodded slowly. 'It's no secret which year I'm in.'

'Were you at that party?'

'I think you should get out.' There was a new rage in Herjólfur's voice, and he was on his feet. 'Barging in here, waking me up … with these crazy accusations.'

'So I take it that means yes?' Ari Thór said firmly.

'What?'

'That you were at the party.'

Ari Thór waited patiently, allowing the boy some time to understand the seriousness of his position. At the same time, he thought through his next move, and how he could break down the resistance, make a way through the heavy defences with which Herjólfur had barricaded himself.

'Quick with his fists, was he?' Ari Thór asked gently.

Herjólfur looked thunderstruck by the question and fear could be seen in his expression for the first time. He shook his head.

'Did your sister get the same treatment?'

'No,' Herjólfur said, with a sigh.

'Your mother?' He asked.

Herjólfur made no reply.

'You're going to have to work with us,' Ari Thór told him in a comforting voice. 'It's the only way out of this.'

After a long silence, Herjólfur nodded his head. 'Yeah. He'd hit her when the mood was on him.'

'She injured her leg skiing?'

'He pushed her over. She fractured her leg when she fell.'

Herjólfur sank down onto the sofa. 'He broke or fractured her leg once before, I think,' he said at last. 'She said she had a fall from a horse not long after they got to know each other. I don't believe it. He was always hitting her.'

The boy looked at the floor and avoided Ari Thór's eyes. Talk of violence in his home had taken him off guard, and he seemed numb with shock.

'And that year's leave that your father took to look after her, was that after a similar incident?'

'What? No ... you've got it wrong,' Herjólfur said. 'She wasn't sick.'

'Really?'

'It was Dad who was on sick leave. He had spells of depression, but it wasn't something that anyone was allowed to mention. Everything was fine on the surface, the perfect policeman on the outside. He never got to the top. Hidden defects. But they still looked after him, made sure he never lost his job. His father's boy, you get me?'

Tómas had described the boy's grandfather, the older Herjólfur's father, as a living legend, an old-school copper.

'Your grandfather's dead, isn't he?'

'Yes, but I don't think he ever really disappeared from Dad's life.'

'But the job was handed down?'

'It's all inherited, unfortunately,' Herjólfur said and Ari Thór could see the effort it was taking him to talk about it. 'Grandad used to knock my grandmother around as well.'

'And your father's violence towards your mother took place over a long period?'

'Far too long,' the boy said heavily. 'Mum's free now. She's a good person.'

'So you did it for her?' Ari Thór asked, without any note of accusation in his voice.

The following silence was a long one and Ari Thór felt a wave of sympathy for the young man, who was clearly deciding whether to leave things as they were, or confess.

Herjólfur finally took a deep breath and spoke carefully.

'To an extent, yes, of course. Someone had to do it. My sister couldn't stand it any longer, so she moved south as soon as she could and never spoke to the old man again. She didn't even come home when we told her about his injuries. The burden landed on me. Otherwise this never would have ended.'

He seemed calm, at peace.

Ari Thór was about to interrupt, to ask for details, but Herjólfur continued without paying Ari Thór any attention.

'But mostly I did it for myself, I think. To break the vicious circle.'

Silence fell again. Ari Thór was reluctant to interrupt the boy's concentration and kept quiet as Herjólfur carried on.

'And I didn't really expect to get away with it. I didn't really care. It's fine as it is. It'll be a blow to my mother when she finds out. The point of it was not to be like him, not to be like my grandfather. It had to end somewhere ... I saw Dad all too often as he turned into a ... a monster. After a while I figured out that this was the only way out. I had to stop him once and for all.'

'You took Ingólfur's shotgun?'

'Yes.'

'And where is it now?'

'It's in a garden shed here in the street.'

'You were going to keep it there?'

'No, it's a summer house, sort of. The place belongs to people who live down south and only come up here in the summer when the weather's good.' He smiled awkwardly. 'I was going to drop it in the sea later, when the fuss had died down.'

'And how did you get your father to go up there?'

'I phoned him. I used a pay-as-you-go SIM card in my phone instead of my own card.'

'He didn't know who was calling?'

'No, he didn't recognise me. I kept my voice low and mumbled, told him there were some druggies up to something in that house. That was enough.'

It was a terrible thought that the boy had led his father into a deadly trap, and Ari Thór wondered if this was the work of a cold-blooded killer or someone who was suffering from some sort of an illness.

'I did shed a few tears,' Herjólfur said in a voice so low that Ari Thór had to listen hard to hear his words. 'I had tears in my eyes as

I fired, not because I was fond of him. Quite the opposite, I hated him deeply. But I cried for him all the same and I don't know why. It was a hard thing to do,' he said and Ari Thór shivered.

'Do you regret it?'

'Regret it?' Herjólfur seemed to need no time to think over his reply. 'No. My mother is free. I'm free as well. Maybe I'll go to prison, but that's fine.'

His eyes were distant and he was clearly somewhere far away from the living room in Siglufjördur.

'Why now?' Ari Thór asked, more for curiosity's sake than for necessity.

'What do you mean?'

'Why did you decide to do this now?'

'It was the diary,' Herjólfur whispered.

'Diary?'

'I found an old diary, came across it by accident. I recognised Dad's handwriting straightaway.'

He sat quietly, his breath coming in heavy gasps.

'It was from 1982, when he was about the age I am now. It took a few days to read it. I didn't really want to get to know him too well, I hated him so much … But when I'd finished reading his entries, I was scared, terrified … He reminded me so much of myself. So I had to do something.'

'And you decided to kill him.'

'To stop him,' Herjólfur said, as if correcting a fundamental mistake. 'You know what he did? He was twenty-two when he wrote the diary … You know how he reacted when he saw he was going the same way as my grandfather?'

Ari Thór shook his head.

'He tried to kill himself, and it obviously wasn't a successful attempt. Grandad had him put in a psychiatric ward. Grandad always got his way, just the same as Dad did later. And I think his time there made things even worse.'

'A psychiatric ward.' The words chimed with Ari Thór, touching on something in his distant memory. Had he overlooked anything in this investigation?

There was a long silence.

'You know, I wish he had been successful,' Herjólfur said at long last. 'The suicide attempt, I mean. That would have been the best thing. The best thing for everyone.'

⊕

Herjólfur went without protest to the police station with Ari Thór. He had asked for the diary before they left the house and Herjólfur willingly handed it over, as if he were glad to be rid of it.

Ari Thór called Tómas and between them they took Herjólfur's formal statement. He confirmed everything he had told Ari Thór, freely confessing to the assault and without any apparent fear of the consequences.

It was obvious that Tómas was relieved that the case was resolved. Ari Thór felt the same way, although he still found it difficult to accept that a boy of nineteen could be responsible for a killing. A turbulent flood of emotions raced through his mind in response to the repugnant thought that the boy could have murdered his own father.

He suddenly remembered why the words 'psychiatric ward' had nagged at him, refusing to be forgotten in the speed of events. It was that call; the call from the woman who had never finished her story. Hadn't she been a *nurse* on a psychiatric ward? He checked back to the log, and there it was. Her name and phone number.

'Ása?' Ari Thór enquired, when she answered the phone.

'Yes,' she replied cautiously.

'Good morning. My name's Ari Thór Arason and I'm a police officer in Siglufjördur.'

'Police officer…?'

'You called us recently about someone who was on the psychiatric ward? You had something to tell us?'

'Well, yes … I'm sorry to have bothered you. It wasn't anything.'

'No problem. But would you be so kind as to tell me the story anyway? Any information, however insignificant, is always useful.'

'I don't doubt that, at least in this instance,' she said. 'Anyhow, I was watching the TV news and saw a face there that I couldn't fail to recognise. The policeman who died.'

'Exactly. Herjólfur,' Ari Thór confirmed, recalling that the photograph used in the news coverage was of a much younger Herjólfur, probably dating back several decades.

'I remembered him from when he was one of my patients, many years ago. I wasn't sure if I should tell you this, and that's why I ended the call. We're bound by confidentiality rules … But it's important to help. After all, the man was murdered,' she said and paused. 'It was all very strange. I found out not long after he was discharged that there were no records of his stay, and I don't know why. He was quite badly unbalanced at the time, I remember that clearly, and we didn't get on well together.' She hesitated before continuing. 'Maybe that was partly my fault, as well. I was still young and took decisions too quickly.'

'Thank you, Ása. This is all very interesting,' Ari Thór said amiably, willing her to continue.

'Good. Pleased to hear it,' the woman replied. 'I was surprised to hear that he had joined the police. I hadn't expected that he would stay on that side of the law, if you see what I mean? He was quick to anger, a troubled young man. I thought you might like to know, especially as all the records of him disappeared. I thought it was very strange at the time…'

'Exactly,' Ari Thór said.

'Well … yes. I've thought of him now and again over the years. I'm sorry to hear how it turned out for him.'

When the call was over, Ari Thór picked up the diary. Tómas had asked him to read it to get as clear a picture as possible before they went in front of the judge in Akureyri to request custody.

It was a dog-eared, old book. The writing was faded but still legible. He felt uncomfortable looking through the man's diary like this, even though he was dead. But he had to read it all the same, and he was curious to know what the contents would show him.

He sat down to read.

July 1982

At last they gave me a pencil and a notebook.

It's an old yellow pencil, badly sharpened, and an old notebook that someone has already used, the first few pages untidily ripped out. Had someone else already tried to put into words their difficulties and their helplessness, just as I'm doing? Maybe there were some pretty doodles there, the unchanging view of the back garden rendered in artistic form, if that could be done. Some things are so grey and cold that no amount of colour on a page could ever bring them to life.

I feel a little better now that I can scribble a few words on paper and I can't explain exactly why. I've never taken any particular satisfaction from writing. It's only now that I have the feeling that this might save my life.

It probably doesn't even matter what I write here in this notebook. Maybe something of the background to my being here, my feelings and this monotonous existence here. Whatever it takes to maintain my sanity.

Epilogue

Spring

Sometimes Ari Thór let his heart, and his pride, run away with him, and he was more than aware of this flaw in himself. He'd allow his emotions to gain the upper hand.

The sun had returned to the little town, getting brighter by the day, although as often as not the cold wind off the sea would still overwhelm any warmth that its rays provided.

With the brighter days had come his promotion to inspector; at last, the long-awaited advancement in his career. While everything was quiet these days – a little too quiet – he certainly enjoyed the title, the influence and the authority that had also allowed him to appoint two subordinates. Changes had also taken place at the municipal offices. Elín had been charged with Valberg's murder, and Gunnar rapidly vacated the position of mayor by 'mutual agreement'. Rumour suggested that he had moved to Norway to be with his family. Ottó had become the new mayor.

But the wind had swept Kristín and Stefnir away from Ari Thór.

Of course some of the blame was his. Because of that damned jealousy, he found it too hard to forgive, and when his anger had finally abated, she had already gone.

Next weekend was a dad's weekend.

But he hadn't given up all hope, far from it.

Their relationship had always been a volatile one.

He needed to sit down with her, find the right moment. He felt an obligation to save his family, if only for Stefnir's sake. Ari Thór had enjoyed a wonderful family life before he lost his parents, and he

wanted Stefnir to experience the same – to have both of his parents
with him throughout his life. Herjólfur's story of recurring domestic violence through the generations had reminded him how good
things were for him – for him, Kristín and Stefnir. He would be a
fool to throw that away.

Maybe he would have to tell her about his father, tell her the real
story behind his mysterious disappearance. As far as she knew, his
father had simply vanished without a trace. But there was far more
to it than that, and Ari Thór had uncovered the truth. He had kept
it from Kristín, and everyone else, but the time had come for them
to have no secrets.

He had hooked her once, and then again, the woman he loved
above all else. Why not third time lucky?

Author's note

As always, I owe a debt of gratitude to the many people who have contributed in one way or another to making *Nightblind* possible. My wife, María Margrét Jóhannsdóttir, and my two daughters, Kira and Natalía (to whom this book is dedicated), provide me with inspiration and support, as do my parents, Jónas Ragnarsson and Katrín Guðjónsdóttir, and my brother, Tómas Jónasson. The kind people of Siglufjördur have also been very supportive, in spite of the growing number of fictional murders taking place in their wonderful town. My warmest thanks also go to my Icelandic publishing team, Pétur Már Ólafsson and Bjarni Þorsteinsson, who have made the Dark Iceland series possible, my publisher Karen Sullivan and translator Quentin Bates, who have both put so much effort into making the series available to English-speaking readers, and my agents, Monica Gram at Copenhagen Literary Agency and David Headley at DHH Literary Agency.

I would also especially like to acknowledge my late grandfather and namesake, Þ. Ragnar Jónasson, who has inspired me through his writing about Siglufjördur. In *Nightblind*, readers hear about the period from mid-November until late January when the sun disappears behind the high Siglufjördur mountains. No one has written about this more beautifully than my grandfather, in a chapter from one of his books on Siglufjördur, *Siglfirskir söguþættir* (*Stories from Siglufjördur*), which was originally written in 1980 and published in 1997. I would like to take this opportunity to include the passage below.

'Spring Returns to the Valley'
by Þ. Ragnar Jónasson (1913–2003)

The winter solstice approaches. The midwinter gloom engulfs the town. As the days pass, it lasts a little longer, but there's light to work by during the daytime hours. Where the sun can be seen, it has little impact. Its rays are almost horizontal and their brightness lasts only a short while.

The writer of these words sits by the window, watching the afternoon's darkness. Outside, the snow falls bitter and cold, as it piles up into drifts, where the clean, sharp, soft powder sparkles.

Indoors, it is warm and cosy. These days it is no longer the fire in the hearth and the oil lamps that provide us with warmth, light and peace of mind, but instead the heat comes from hot springs in Skútudalur valley and electricity from the turbines at Skeidsfoss waterfall. Technology adds comfort to our lives.

There is no gleam of sunshine to light up the inside of the high ring of mountains that encircles Siglufjördur. The winter sun disappeared, as usual, behind Blekkilsfjall mountain on the 15th of November. After that there is only a faint glow to be seen on the Hafnarhyrna and Hestsskardshnjúkur mountains, if it is clear enough in the middle of the day. There is only a sudden flash of reflected sunshine that passes between the peaks before the day's brightness fades up here in the far north of the world.

The high moon shines at night, sending its enchanting brightness over the white winter lands, where there is hardly a blemish to be seen. Midnight-blue shadows fill the fissures and chasms. An endless variety of glittering greys and silvers make the landscape both indistinct and mysterious. The waters of the fjord surge in the light of the moon and the scintillating northern lights adorn the dark blue bowl of the heavens with their magnificent display.

With the passing of the solstice on the 21st to 22nd of December, the light returns, gradually but steadily. The days stretch by a bird's footstep at a time, until the sun visits again on the 28th of January, the day of the sun. The bright beauty of the winter sun reaches over Hólshyrna mountain, after an absence of seventy-four days and then the town has cause to celebrate.

The Úlfsdalafjöll peaks to the west, and to the east the headland of Siglunesmúli and the Stadarhóls mountains have long provided shelter for the people of Siglufjördur, when bitter weather rages elsewhere across the land and the northern seas. But during the gloom of the year's shortest days, when the biting northerly storms fling snow around Nesnúpur and into Siglufjördur, and then further inside the ring of mountains, there are those who feel that the world is closing in around them. Harsh weather and arctic darkness are a trial for everyone's inner strength. Others relish this time of year, which they feel is the best of all for relaxation, rest and exercising the mind.

After the great flood many years ago, God made a covenant with old Noah. 'While the earth remaineth, seedtime and harvest, and cold and heat, and summer and winter, and day and night shall not cease.' And God put his rainbow in the sky to stand witness to their covenant.

The seasons follow their set course, with sunshine giving way to showers. As always the sweet is blended with the sour. Each follows the other, good and ill, the optimism of spring and the anxiousness that precedes winter, and always lit by the brightness of a new day after the darkness of night, as Freysteinn Gunnarsson says in his poem:

Though storm and dread rage,
No one should be fearful.
Always
The light shall return,
As spring returns to the valley.

The joys of summer and the delights that nature brings will again be with us in this town so far north. The rays of the sun gild the mountain slopes in the calm weather of the bright season, making the whole fjord a box of sunshine.

The nightless summer months adorn the mountains and the valleys with myriad colours and the sea rests as calm as a pool of golden oil, morning and evening. What can equal the placid stillness and loveliness of an early summer morning when the stately mountains with their slopes so green are reflected in the fjord, so sensitive to beauty?

Then all the ills of winter are swept away.

An exclusive extract from Ragnar Jónasson's Blackout, *translated by Quentin Bates and coming soon from Minotaur Books.*

PART ONE

SUMMER

How do you like Iceland?

That, at the very least, was the kind of question he had come to Iceland to avoid.

The day began well, as the fine June morning dawned. Not that there was any evident difference between morning and evening at this time of year, when the sun stayed bright around the clock, casting blinding light wherever he looked. Evan Fein had long anticipated visiting this island at the edge of the habitable world.

It was this Ohio art history student's first visit to Iceland. Nature had pooled its energies, as if to add to the woes of the financial crash, by presenting Icelanders with two volcanic eruptions, one right after the other. The volcanic activity appeared to have subsided, for the moment, and Evan had just missed the events. He had spent a few days in Iceland, starting by taking in the sights of Reykjavík and the tourist spots around the city. Then he hired a car and set off for the north. After a night at the campsite at Blönduós, he made an early start, setting out for Skagafjördur. He had purchased a CD of old-fashioned Icelandic ballads and slotted it into the car's player, enjoying the music without understanding a word of the lyrics, proud to be something of a travel nerd, immersing himself in the culture of the countries he visited. He took the winding Thverárfjall road, turning off before he got as far as the town of Saudarkrókur on the far side of the peninsula. He wanted to take a look at Gréttir's Bath, the stone-flagged hot thermal pool that he knew had to be somewhere nearby, not far from the shore.

It was a slow drive along the rutted track to the pool, and he wondered if trying to find it was a waste of time. But the thought of relaxing for a while in the steaming water and taking in both the beauty of his surroundings and the tranquillity of the morning was a tempting one. He drove at a snail's pace, lambs scattering from the sides of the road as he passed, but the pool stubbornly refused to be found. Evan started to wonder if he had missed the turning, and slowed down at every farm gate, trying to work out if the entrance to the pool might be hidden away – across a farmer's land, or down a side turning, a country lane. Had he driven too far? Then he saw a handsome house that on closer inspection looked to be half-built. It stood not far from the road with a small grey van parked in front of it. He pulled his car to the side of the road, and stopped. Something looked odd.

The driver, or the house's owner, perhaps, was lying on the ground near the house. Unmoving. Unconscious? Evan started with surprise, unbuckling his seatbelt and opening the door without even turning off the engine. The age-old ballads continued to crackle from the car's tinny speakers, making the scene almost surreal.

Evan started to run, but then slowed as the man came into view. He was dead. There was no doubt about that.

It had to be a man lying there, judging by the build and the cropped hair. There was no chance of identifying the face, which was erased by a spatter of blood.

Where there had once been an eye, there was now an empty socket.

He gasped for air and stared numbly at the corpse in front of him, fumbling for his phone, the incongruous sound of his Icelandic ballads in the background.

He turned quickly, checking that the man's assailant wasn't behind him. *Nothing.*

Apart from the dead man, Evan was alone. Next to the body was a length of timber, smeared with blood. The weapon? Evan retched and he tried to stifle the thoughts that flooded his mind. *Think. Be calm.* He sat down beside the pasture in front of the house, and punched out the emergency number on his phone, wishing fervently that he had picked another destination for his holiday.

Iceland is one of the safest places on earth, said the travel guide.

Evan's eyes darted around, taking in the warm summer sun casting her glow across the verdant fields, the stunning mountains hovering in the distance, the glint of her rays on the bright-blue waters of the outlying fjord and its magnificent islands.

Not anymore, he thought, as the operator was connected.

Not anymore.